LORD OF ATLANTIS

Borgo Press Books by JOHN RUSSELL FEARN

1,000-Year Voyage: A Science Fiction Novel * *Anjani the Mighty: A Lost Race Novel* (Anjani #2) * *Black Maria, M.A.: A Classic Crime Novel* (Black Maria #1) * *The Crimson Rambler: A Crime Novel* * *Don't Touch Me: A Crime Novel* * *Dynasty of the Small: Classic Science Fiction Stories* * *The Empty Coffins: A Mystery of Horror* * *The Fourth Door: A Mystery Novel* * *From Afar: A Science Fiction Mystery* * *Fugitive of Time: A Classic Science Fiction Novel* * *The G-Bomb: A Science Fiction Novel* * *The Genial Dinosaur* (Herbert the Dinosaur #2) * *The Gold of Akada: A Jungle Adventure Novel* (Anjani #1) * *Here and Now: A Science Fiction Novel* * *Into the Unknown: A Science Fiction Tale* * *Last Conflict: Classic Science Fiction Stories* * *Legacy from Sirius: A Classic Science Fiction Novel* * *The Man from Hell: Classic Science Fiction Stories* * *The Man Who Was Not: A Crime Novel* * *Manton's World: A Classic Science Fiction Novel* * *Moon Magic: A Novel of Romance* (as Elizabeth Rutland) * *The Murdered Schoolgirl: A Classic Crime Novel* (Black Maria #2) * *One Remained Seated: A Classic Crime Novel* (Black Maria #3) * *One Way Out: A Crime Novel* (with Philip Harbottle) * *Pattern of Murder: A Classic Crime Novel* * *Reflected Glory: A Dr. Castle Classic Crime Novel* * *Robbery Without Violence: Two Science Fiction Crime Stories* * *Rule of the Brains: Classic Science Fiction Stories* * *Shattering Glass: A Crime Novel* * *The Silvered Cage: A Scientific Murder Mystery* * *Slaves of Ijax: A Science Fiction Novel* * *Something from Mercury: Classic Science Fiction Stories* * *The Space Warp: A Science Fiction Novel* * *A Thing of the Past* (Herbert the Dinosaur #1) * *Thy Arm Alone: A Classic Crime Novel* (Black Maria #4) * *The Time Trap: A Science Fiction Novel* * *Vision Sinister: A Scientific Detective Thriller* * *Voice of the Conqueror: A Classic Science Fiction Novel* * *What Happened to Hammond? A Scientific Mystery* * *Within That Room!: A Classic Crime Novel*

THE GOLDEN AMAZON SAGA

1. *World Beneath Ice* * 2. *Lord of Atlantis* * 3. *Triangle of Power* * 4. *The Amethyst City* * 5. *Daughter of the Amazon* * 6. *Quorne Returns* * 7. *The Central Intelligence* * 8. *The Cosmic Crusaders* * 9. *Parasite Planet* * 10. *World Out of Step* * 11. *The Shadow People* * 12. *Kingpin Planet* * 13. *World in Reverse* * 14. *Dwellers in Darkness* * 15. *World in Duplicate* * 16. *Lords of Creation* * 17. *Duel with Colossus* * 18. *Standstill Planet* * 19. *Ghost World* * 20. *Earth Divided* * 21. *Chameleon Planet* (with Philip Harbottle)

LORD OF ATLANTIS

THE GOLDEN AMAZON SAGA, BOOK TWO

JOHN RUSSELL FEARN

Edited by Philip Harbottle

THE BORGO PRESS

MMXII

LORD OF ATLANTIS

FIRST BORGO PRESS EDITION

Published by Wildside Press LLC

www.wildsidebooks.com

DEDICATION

For Bob Madle

CONTENTS

THE GOLDEN AMAZON
by Philip Harbottle

In 1943 British writer John Russell Fearn decided to quit writing for the American pulp science fiction magazines, and to concentrate instead on books for the English market. Within a very few years he became established as a leading novelist in several genres, not only science fiction, but also mystery and detective fiction, and westerns.

His first new SF novel, *The Golden Amazon*, was published by World's Work in April 1944. In this story, a little girl of three years of age is made the subject of an idealistic scientist's illegal glandular experiments. The scientist's dream is to end world wars by creating a woman devoid of the usual lusts and frailties of mankind, who upon reaching maturity would institute a benign scientific rule. But the apparently successful experiment has a flaw: it instills into the girl a hatred for all men, and a ruthless cruelty. Her supernatural scientific gifts enable her to master atomic power, and practically leads her to destroy the world. She breaks the will and strength of men, and elevates women to positions of wealth and power. She also discovers human synthesis, and by this means she is able to escape retribution when she is eventually overthrown. She is seen to collapse and die, a victim of consuming ketabolism, echoing the memorable finale of Rider Haggard's *She*. In actuality, it was only her synthetic image, and this paved the way for the *Golden Amazon Returns*, and further sequels

Fearn sold reprint rights in the first novel to the prestigious Canadian magazine, the Toronto *Star Weekly*. The magazine carried a special Comics Supplement, the centre section of which was a 'complete novel', published in newspaper format. Aimed at a general readership, the novels were written by the top popular novelists of the day, including John Dickson Carr, Ellery Queen, and P. G. Wodehouse. They sold hundreds of thousands of copies, and the novels were syndicated to several American newspapers in the Maine and New York areas. The Amazon novels enjoyed extraordinary popularity (especially with Canadian housewives), and ran for the next sixteen years following the appearance of the first novel in the March 3, 1945 issue, ending with Fearn's sudden death in September 1960, aged only fifty-two. His final two Amazon novels appeared posthumously.

During Fearn's lifetime, only the first six novels were published in British hardcover editions from the World's Work in England, after appearing in the *Star Weekly*. This was because the publishers discontinued their entire fiction line in 1954. However, the Amazon novels continued to appear in the *Star Weekly*, eventually notching up twenty-four titles.

Fearn had resold paperback rights to the Canadian publisher Harlequin Books, but after publishing only the first three titles, they stopped publishing SF and other genre fiction to concentrate on their famous Romances line.

Meanwhile, as early as 1949, Fearn had realized that the Amazon series had the potential to run indefinitely. This presented him with a problem, however. The 'origin story' of the Golden Amazon was conceived and actually set during the Second World War. Subsequent novels were written during the war and the immediate postwar period, and projected their stories only a few decades into the future.

He very astutely realized that to keep ahead of reality, he needed to move the Amazon *further* into the future—first into the outer solar system, and thence to the stars. So with the seventh novel, he introduced a new main character, Abna of Atlantis—someone as equally intelligent, and even stronger than herself. These dynamics provided him with an *interstellar* canvas, thus ensuring that the series would remain ahead of reality.

Fearn's strategy was a great success, and the Amazon novels retained their popularity, ending only with his tragically early death in 1960. By then he had written a further twenty Amazon novels, and made preliminary notes for his next (which would later be written by Fearn's biographer, Philip Harbottle).

Long after Fearn's death, his entire Amazon series

would eventually see print from the pioneering US small press Gryphon Books in limited paperback editions, and later by the Canadian Battered Silicon Dispatch Box small press in their hardcover Omnibus series.

This new Borgo paperback series will be the first trade edition of all twenty-one of these later novels by Fearn, beginning with the seventh novel in the original series. First published in 1949 as *Conquest of the Amazon*, I have edited it slightly as *World Beneath Ice* (The Golden Amazon Saga, Book One) so that it can be read and enjoyed by new readers who may be totally unfamiliar with what had gone before. Subsequent novels have also been slightly edited for modern readers.

The publishers hope that this new series may create many more "fans of the Amazon." Meanwhile, any reader interested in seeking out the earlier six Golden Amazon novels will find that they are readily available on the internet, and in numerous earlier paperback and hardcover editions.

* * * * * *

To date, readers can enjoy the following new Borgo editions:

Book One: *World Beneath Ice*

In destroying the threat of an alien invasion, the Golden Amazon had inadvertently caused a decline in the sun's heat, encasing Earth in an ice sheet that threatens to eliminate humanity. The Amazon encounters Abna, a descendant of Atlantis, stronger and even more scientifically advanced than she, and the ruler of an Atlantean colony still surviving in a protected environment on Jupiter. She refuses his offer of marriage, but agrees to form an alliance in order to restore the sun and save the Earth. One thing that Abna has not told the Amazon is that all the females of his race have been wiped out by a bacilli infection....

CHAPTER ONE
UPHEAVAL

Commander Ronald Clifton, chief navigator of the space-liner *Atom Cloud*, stood gazing out of the big observation window of the bridge. He was looking at something he could not quite understand, something that did not fit into his years of experience in the space-ways between Earth and Mars. Presently he turned, speaking in his clipped voice.

"Have you a moment, Mr. Claxton?" The second navigator glanced up from studying his instruments and moved to his superior's side. The commander motioned through the window. "What the blazes do you imagine that is?" he asked.

Claxton gazed steadily. Here in the utter depths of space, some millions of miles from Earth—from which the liner was heading in the direction of Mars—a most unusual spacecraft was visible. In these sheer distances where no air intervened, where the sun blazed with relentless, blinding glory, it was hard to estimate mileage.

The object at which both men were staring was probably 3,000 miles away—an enormous wheel, it seemed.

"Not the least idea, sir," Claxton said. "Looks a bit like one of those alien spacecraft we had trouble with some time ago."

"Can't be that; they were all destroyed by the Golden Amazon. Anyway, that thing is much bigger. Get the reflector set up, Mr. Claxton."

"Right, sir." The second navigator turned to the powerful telescopic apparatus and adjusted its light-trapping devices and screens so that it was prismatically reflecting the distant object onto a broad viewing screen. The Commander gazed at it and gave a long whistle of surprise.

"Not a disc, sir, as we thought," Claxton said. "It's a globe of some sort with glass circles all around it."

"Yes—if that's what they are," the Commander said. "They might even be lenses of great size. Sixteen of them circling that ball like a necklace. There seems to be windows in the ball, too. I certainly never saw anything like it before. Apparently it's heading in the direction of Earth."

"Might be dangerous," Claxton suggested. "Do you think we ought to warn them back home? They're in no shape for meeting any possible menace while rebuilding everything from the great glacier catastrophe."

"It's not our job to issue warnings, Mr. Claxton. That's a panic action. We'll report what we have seen and leave it at that. Attend to it, will you?"

"Immediately, sir." The Commander returned his

attention to the big window. It was his responsibility to get this huge liner safely to Mars, not conjecture on the meaning of a strange spacecraft. Nevertheless, he did wonder quite a lot about it as he watched its glittering circle slowly sink into the abyss in the direction of far-flung Earth.

On Earth itself the information concerning the weird craft did not excite undue attention, chiefly because those in charge of world affairs had more than enough on their minds in restoring order after chaos. Only a few months had passed since the whole world had been encased in a cocoon of ice—the Great Glacier, as it had been called—created by the near death of the Sun. That the Sun now blazed again upon the world and surrounding planets, as hot and friendly as of yore, was entirely owing to the combined sciences of Violet Ray Brant—the Golden Amazon—and Abna, a descendant of the lost city of Atlantis, whose home now lay beneath the distant Red Spot of Jupiter. The Amazon herself, acclaimed at last throughout the world for her stupendous feat in rekindling the orb of day, had virtually become dictatress of Earthly policy. Since she had always taken a leading part in world affairs, especially when scientific problems arose, her rise to absolute power really signified but little. She was pleased—and nothing more—that the Earth's inhabitants had at last decided to elect her of their own volition; otherwise nothing was changed.

Day by day she sat in the headquarters of central London, from where came all the world's orders, discussing plans with engineers and architects for rebuilding, arranging new social levels, planning endlessly to bring an ordered, beautiful world out of the chaos left by the glacier. Parts of London were already rebuilt. The Dodd Space Line to other worlds was operating again, chiefly so that reconstruction could begin on other planets as well, they also having suffered severely from the sun's near-extinction.

When the news of the strange craft reached the Amazon, she sat studying its details outlined in the report, oblivious for the moment of the helpers on either side of her.

There was Chris Wilson, Chief Executive of the Dodd Space Line—a fleshy, pink-faced man verging on late middle age. Next to him, musing over a new social outline for the youth of the world, was his daughter Ethel, close on thirty, black-haired, blue-eyed, intensely vital and alert. Farther along the conference table sat Beatrice Wilson, mellow and middle-aged, Ethel's mother; and opposite her were Commander and Ruth Kerrigan, formerly Dodd, the owners of the space line.

The Amazon handed the report to Wilson without comment. The passing years, so marked now in the elderly members present, did not exist for her, She still looked about twenty-five, graceful as a tigress, amber-skinned, her beautiful face unmarred by a single line. The scarlet in which she was dressed emphasized the flowing gold of her shoulder-length hair and the deep purple of her eyes. Even had her attractiveness been that of beauty alone, it would have been fascinating—but this was her least vital gift. Her power lay in her superhuman strength and uncanny scientific knowledge, both gifts wished on her by the skill of a long dead surgeon during her infancy. Chris Wilson, handing the report to his neighbour, said: "We've nothing like that in the spaceways."

"No, we haven't." The Amazon sat musing, her gaze fixed absently through the vast window onto the girders and skeletal buildings of reviving London. "And we also know that the colonists on the Moon and Mars have not. Mercury is dead, Venus is completely uninhabitable. So this craft is either from some unknown spot in the void and contains explorers—or, more likely, it has come from Jupiter."

Ethel Wilson gave a start. "Aunt Vi, you mean it might be Abna, that god-like man who helped you rekindle the Sun? The one who once saved me from death?"

"Yes, it might be Abna," the Amazon agreed, and smiled a trifle cynically to herself. "It wouldn't be a great surprise, either. He never did strike me as being the kind of man to take a beating lying down."

"I think you did wrongly toward Abna, Vi," Chris Wilson said. "After all, he had much to give—vast science derived from Atlantis—and all he wanted in return was for you to marry him. Instead of that, you palmed a synthetic image of yourself onto him and let him go back home!"

"He deceived me, so I deceived him." The Amazon

raised and lowered her graceful shoulders. "He only wanted marriage with me for one purpose—because not a single woman exists in his race, inhabiting the domed city under the Red Spot of Jupiter. His idea was to marry me, our offspring to form the basis of a new race. Coldly scientific and biological. It had nothing to do with his professed love for me."

"I can't quite believe that, Vi," Commander Kerrigan said, smiling in his wealth of grey beard. "I could not imagine a better matched pair than you and Abna. He's every bit as scientific as you are and, surprisingly enough, every bit as strong. You are sure it isn't jealousy of his power and intelligence that makes you pretend to hate him?"

"I don't hate him, and I never said I did. He deserved teaching a lesson for hoodwinking me. If it should be he who has returned, I'm afraid he'll have to learn yet another lesson. As I told him in my concluding words, it will have to be his science against mine."

She glanced about her at a gradually deepening vibration. The sensation increased until the room, for a moment, seemed to sway and then became steady again.

"That," Chris said, "was a mighty big earth shock somewhere!"

The Amazon nodded, undisturbed. "Not that it's anything unusual these days. Earthquakes following the collapse of the great glacier are inevitable."

* * * * * * *

At that moment, two transatlantic pilots were viewing the cause of the earthquake from a height of 10,000 feet. Their job was flying the four-a-day rocket plane freight flights across the Atlantic from London to New York. This was the third trip of the day. One moment they were streaking through the pale blue spring sky with nothing disturbing the peace of the rolling Atlantic far beneath; the next they beheld the most incredible thing they had never known.

The grey rollers of the ocean parted mysteriously ahead of them, and Pilot Carson suddenly cut down speed as he saw the phenomenon commencing. "Balls of fire!" he breathed, stunned. "Just take a look at that, Jeff!"

Jeff Baxley, his navigator, did not need to be told. Pop-eyed, he was gazing at the waters, agitated by some invisible and inconceivably powerful force, as they rolled upward and outward before the arrival of something from the ocean's depths. At the same moment, violent air disturbances and a sense of tremendous magnetic strain hit the flier.

It swayed and reeled out of control, spun about in a vast electrical vortex.

Dazed, but still unhurt, unable to control the craft, the two men watched land, buried for centuries under the ocean, start rising from the water, thrusting algae-covered pinnacles into the sunlight, water pouring from every cranny as though from the conning tower of a surfacing submarine.

The pinnacles became large, pointed rocks—then

rose higher and became hills. Higher still until they were revealed as actual mountains. Land at their bases came next, thrust out of the ocean's depths and stretching in a colossal plateau as far as the pilots could see in either direction.

Then the electrical vortex was gone and they gazed at mighty tidal waves receding from them, one in each direction, which must finally crash on the shores of Britain, Federated Europe, the United States, and perhaps eastern South America.

With difficulty Pilot Carson got the flier under control again. "Dry land!" he cried. "Just look at it, Jeff! Dry land where there was ocean—a huge plateau of it! I'll bet it goes all the way from Britain to America across the Atlantic."

Jeff switched on recording cameras, and changing direction, Carson set the machine flying over the dripping rock landscape where formerly the Atlantic had rolled in majesty. Everywhere the two men looked there were lakes, still draining off into the depths of the plateau. Where the water had already vanished there were endless acres of green algae and sea fungi. The most incredible things of all were the mountains towering into the sky.

Carson said, "The tops of those mountains were originally the islands of the Azores. Now they're sticking nearly 3,000 feet into the air."

The navigator said, staring ahead intently, "Looks to me like a city or something, under a glass cover."

As the flier swept onward there loomed up a mighty

gleaming hemisphere, entirely devoid of algae and catching the light of the sun in a myriad reflections. It rose perhaps 300 feet at the highest point—a perfect dome.

Carson swung the flier so that they swept over it in a circle, the cameras recording steadily. There certainly was some kind of city inside the dome, but of people or life of any kind there was no trace. In fact, there was more than a city under the dome. There seemed to be quite a lot of forest as well.

"That's the biggest saucepan lid I ever saw," Carson said. "Must be all of thirty miles across at its base. We'll finish our hop and then tip them off with the information in London. Good job we have a camera record, otherwise they'd think us crazy." The machine darted westward to continue its course toward the United States. It appeared that a link had been born uniting Britain and Federated Europe with the American continent.

The havoc caused by the initial earthquake itself, followed by the vast tidal waves that crashed in on the shores of the United States and Britain, was sufficient to cause inquiry in all directions. To the Golden Amazon it became a matter of paramount importance to discover what had happened. Though central London had survived the full fury of the tidal wave which had come up the Thames, a great deal of it was under water, and the new building projects had been destroyed to the accompaniment of a heavy death toll.

It was an hour after the initial earthquake that the

tidal wave arrived, and for another two hours after that, well into the afternoon, the Amazon was busy at her communications desk, asking for details of the disaster. In the office with her there still remained Chris Wilson, his wife, and Ethel. The Kerrigans had departed to their own executive offices.

"As far as I can make out," the Amazon said finally, "there is something abnormal out in the Atlantic—some kind of land-rise about which the facts are not clear. That, of course, would create a tremendous water displacement that would account for the tidal waves. I suppose I ought to go and look, but with things in their present state I don't see how I can spare the time."

"I can," Ethel offered. "There's a New York air liner leaving in an hour. I could go and see what's taken place, then radio the information back to you. Save a lot of secondhand reports. I could fly my own plane of course, but there are so many climatic upheavals at present I'd prefer the safety of a liner."

"Good enough," the Amazon agreed promptly. "You do that."

Ethel nodded and hurried from the office, and the Amazon said: "A landrise in the Atlantic, coming on top of the report of that globular spacecraft seems remarkably coincidental. If, as I have suspected, it is Abna who has returned, the first thing he would perhaps do would be to try to resurrect the land where his ancestors were born—the continent of Mu, the mountains of which are believed to be the present Azores."

"But Vi, what on earth are you getting at?" Beatrice

Wilson demanded blankly. "You don't mean to say that this man, Abna, has deliberately created all this havoc? He wouldn't! He's not that kind."

The Amazon smiled. "It still takes you a long time to realise the lengths to which some men will go to achieve an object, Bee, doesn't it? Believe me, if Abna was resolved on restoring Mu, and perhaps the lost city of Atlantis itself, he'd not for a moment consider the upheaval caused thereby. Anyway," she added, shrugging, "it's all assumption until we have definite information. Certainly I don't propose to go rushing about to investigate until I get the facts."

Then the automatic speaker in the ceiling made an announcement. "Pilot Carson and Navigator Baxley to see you, Miss Brant. Most urgent communication."

She pressed a button on her desk and the two young men came in. "You have an urgent communication?" the Amazon asked briefly. "Please state it concisely."

"We're just back from New York, Miss Brant," Pilot Carson explained. "Considerable damage has been caused there, and all along the east coast of the Americas, by a tidal wave—damage similar to that caused here."

"Yes, yes, I know that." The Amazon sounded and looked impatient. "I heard of it over the communications system. Have you nothing more important to report?"

"There is dry land, about twenty miles in width, now linking America with Britain, which has resulted in partial submergence of other continents by the displacement of water. There is also a city."

"A city?" The girl's violet eyes sharpened. "Where?"

"Approximately near the middle of this newly created plateau, Miss Brant." Carson gave the details and then added: "We saw the whole thing happen, from the moment this buried land and mountain range rose out of the depths. The mountain peaks used to be called the Azores. I have a filmed record of everything."

"Come into the laboratory where we have better facilities."

The Amazon led the way into a huge adjoining room filled with complicated instruments that she had devised.

In silence the Amazon, Chris, and his wife—the two pilots in the background—stood watching the extraordinary scenes the cameras had recorded.

"Seems to me that Ethel is going to have a trip in vain," Chris said. "She can't usefully add any more to this recording."

The Amazon said: "Let her go, Chris. Something more may have developed by the time she flies over this newly risen continent. Obviously, it is the resurrected Mu, just as I guessed—and that city under the giant dome is lost Atlantis, evidently perfectly preserved from its long immersion in the depths by the dome which has covered it. The spherical shape of the dome would lessen the deep-water pressure. All of which brings me back to one inevitable answer. Abna!"

"Seems like it," Chris admitted. "I can't think of anybody else who could conceivably have any interest in lost Atlantis. Which in turn ties up with the mystery of that spacecraft."

The Amazon turned to the enormous radar telescope in the laboratory. It 'found' its objectives in broad daylight by the radar beam recoiling from a chosen spot in the heavens, the displays showing the size and position of the object. Seating herself at the control board, the Amazon went to work on the keys, her fingers playing up and down them until the beam struck the object for which she was seeking. She studied the readings and calculated swiftly. "That must be it," she said finally. "It is 20,000 miles from Earth and moving in a slow orbit around Earth. Nothing else in that space location, so it isn't a meteorite. We'll have a look at it."

She switched on the motors controlling the telescope and set the guider that would direct it exactly at the object the radar beam had located. There was an interval as the masterpiece of engineering directed itself, then the viewing screen came to life, mirroring an image of the weird craft.

It shone golden, while around its 'equator' there was ringed the curious-looking mirrors, or lenses. There were also signs of exterior catwalks on the object and the dull gleam of domes that could have been glass conning towers or outlook ports.

For half an hour the Amazon studied it, then with grim face she switched off.

"Seems to be of phenomenal size," she said. "As big as a town and probably equipped with every known scientific device. Abna may be controlling it or he may not. Whoever it is, I'm perfectly sure that the person is responsible for the chaos on Earth here and the resurrection of Atlantis. And it may mean something much more menacing. Why resurrect Atlantis unless it is intended to use it? It doubtless contains many highly scientific engines of destruction, which, turned loose against us, might prove too much even for my science. The original Atlanteans were wizards of science against which my own knowledge might prove puny. I'll fly out to this craft in the *Ultra* and see what I can learn. If it is Abna, maybe I can reason with him. If I can't do that, then I can perhaps destroy him. Whichever course opens, he must be stopped!"

"In other words," Chris said, with a dry smile, "any chance is better than none to have a look at Abna again?"

The Amazon flashed him a stony glance. "Don't underrate the situation, Chris! There's danger there; deadly danger, unless it is crushed at the start. You seem to have forgotten that Abna and I parted as enemies, so we'll remain so. His science or mine. There isn't room in the universe for both of us, and if he dares to invade my territory, I'll wipe him out because I'll have no alternative. Certainly I'll never submit to his dictates." She turned to the door, adding over her shoulder, "Take charge whilst I'm gone, Chris. You know as well as I do how much needs handling. Whatever report Ethel has to make can wait until I get back."

CHAPTER TWO
THREAT FROM SPACE

An hour later the *Ultra*, the huge, super-fast air-and-space machine which the Amazon alone understood in detail, was streaking into the twilight—upward to the stratosphere, thence through successively weakening layers of atmosphere until the machine had plunged through into the void.

It was not a new scene that lay before the girl, or indeed to anybody in these space-conscious days of the late twenty-first century; yet it always had a certain gripping quality. The majestic sun, blinding and intolerable to look upon without intervening purple shields; the drifting hosts of stars and planets; the paler moon, at the first quarter and below the gigantic bulk of Earth, receding now as the *Ultra* swept onward into the abyss.

Motionless, the Amazon sat at the controls, watching through the observation port for the first sign of that golden circle toward which the instruments told her she was speeding.

She was no longer the scarlet-costumed ruler of Earth, queen of the inner solar system, but a black-suited adventuress, the negativity of her attire relieved only by the solid gold belt about her slender waist, a belt packed with every needful instrument and weapon. Such an attire she always wore when on business bent. In any moment of crisis making demands upon her physique, the close-fitting elastic-glass mesh of which the suit was made gave her absolute freedom. Her golden hair was swept back now from her forehead and held in place by a gleaming band with twin rubies at either end. A stray hair in her way when she needed absolute clarity of vision might prove fatal. To the Amazon no detail was too trivial to be overlooked. She had learned from hard experience the need of precision and deadly accuracy.

When presently the golden circle came into view from the depthless black of infinity, she became more alert, her right hand near enough to the protonic gun to press the switch if any attempt was made to attack her. Nothing happened, however, and she flew steadily on.

When she was 20,000 miles from Earth, she inspected the giant space-globe as she flew the *Ultra* around it. The mirrors were concave in shape like the reflector of an arc, and she judged them to be twenty feet in diameter and made of some highly polished substance beside which the most brilliant chrome finish would have seemed dull.

That the craft itself was man-made was no longer in doubt. The rivets that held the globe's two hemispheres together were plainly visible. So were the catwalk ladders and transparent conning towers, behind which she could see dim evidences of people moving—probably watching her *Ultra* as it cruised around like a wasp, darting, diving, sweeping, taking avoiding action in case of attack.

Then suddenly the Amazon found the *Ultra* seized in the grip of tremendous magnetic power. Though she exerted all the strength of the atomic plant to break free, she found it impossible. Relentlessly, the *Ultra* was dragged toward the globe, and finally came to rest anchored against it.

Grim-faced, furious at being beaten, the Amazon switched off the power and looked out of the window. Close to it was the nearest catwalk ladder on the side of the globe, leading up to a closed metal door. Near to the door was a small window through which she could descry the dim outline of a watching face.

She got into a spacesuit and stepped out of the *Ultra*'s safety lock and onto the vessel's roof. The slight mass of the *Ultra* and the much heavier mass of the globe did strange things to her sense of balance. She found herself floating upward with the buoyancy of a feather, her leaded feet kicking in the sheer abyss of space.

Helplessly she turned several somersaults and then with a slight bump she hit the side of the globe. Immediately she caught hold of the ladder rungs, and began to cautiously haul herself up to the metal door. Below her was infinity, depthless, powdered with the sparkling lights of unguessably distant stars. It was a view thar would have affected a normal being from insupportable vertigo—but not the Amazon. In these great wastes of infinity she felt at home.

Reaching the metal door, she hammered upon it with her metal-and-rubber gloved hand, using the other hand to cling to the rail. There was only a moment's interval, then the door opened and she stepped into the blank darkness of an air-valve chamber, so designed that it refilled with air pressure identical to that beyond the second door.

Accustomed to this normal routine in space, she waited in the darkness; then the second door opened and she stepped into a wide control room, brilliantly lighted by the sunlight blazing through the roof conning tower.

Three men were at an enormous control board, all of them lightly dressed in toga-like costumes. Near the massive power generators was a tall, thin-faced man of uncertain age who was watching her closely.

Unlike the men at the control board, he was fully dressed in a costume that looked like cloth-of-gold, ornamented with numberless emblems and decorations. Then the Amazon switched her attention to the tallest man in the room.

He stood almost seven feet and was scantily clad, his folded arms revealing the rippling health of his bronzed skin and the tremendous development of his muscles. He was handsome beyond the ordinary, with pointed features, a resolute chin, and a shock of golden hair in the waves of which the blazing sun lingered. In spite of herself, the Amazon found her gaze fixed by his reddish-blue eyes.

He smiled at her and she promptly stiffened. Just

for a moment she had forgotten she was the Golden Amazon, and had almost become a living, breathing woman. She had only experienced such an emotional upheaval once before, and that had been when she had first met this extraordinarily handsome young man with the frame and features of some mythical Grecian god.

With a quick movement the Amazon unfastened the catch that secured her helmet and tipped the covering back on its hinge to her shoulders. She advanced slowly.

"Abna," she said quietly. "So I guessed correctly."

"I'm glad to see you again, Vi," he responded in his pleasant baritone and he came over to her.

"I cannot say that I can return the compliment," she said.

He considered her. "I suppose it is you this time?" he asked drily. "Not a synthetic model, like the one you foisted on me when we left Mercury?"

"I explained that." The girl swung on him, her violet eyes bright with scorn. "You must have got my communication through the image, explaining my reasons for parting company with you."

"Yes. I got them. But you don't suppose that two such as us—both scientists—could remain parted forever, do you? My first thought when I returned home to Jupiter was to come back and make you realise how mistaken you had been about me."

"You chose a very spectacular method! I hope you feel satisfied, now that you have created a world-wide earthquake, brought Mu from the depths, and drowned thousands of innocent people in tidal waves."

"That," the Atlantean giant said quietly, "is unfortunate. I hardly thought resurrecting Mu would have caused such chaos." He changed the subject abruptly and motioned to the tall, saturnine being with the decorations on his golden raiment.

"This is His Excellency Sefner Quorne," he introduced. "He is my chief adviser. Formerly, he held that position with my father who was, as you may remember, the ruling dignitary of our small race of 3,000 males. Now, unhappily, my father has passed on, and I have taken his place as the ruler of the surviving Atlanteans."

The Amazon nodded but did not say anything. Sefner Quorne bowed toward her with solemn dignity and then straightened again, his heliotrope-coloured eyes watching her with an intensity she did not like.

"Don't you think it's time you explained what this is all about, Abna?" she asked curtly. "You seem to forget that I am the ruler of Earth, and that what happens to Earth people is very much my business. I don't intend to tolerate your having this monstrous vessel of yours here, causing havoc whenever the mood seizes you. What do you intend doing next—take over Atlantis?"

"Why not? It has been drawn from the depths by the simple process of degravitation. A neutralizing beam was directed from this space-globe, which negated gravity around the area of Mu and caused that continent to rise, with Atlantis intact upon it, still sealed as it was at the time of the Deluge. The next step is to destroy the sealing dome that surrounds it. Then we shall come to Earth and restore the scientific amenities of the city."

"I won't allow it!" the Amazon snapped. "It's tantamount to invasion!"

"Maybe, but don't forget we have four-dimensional weapons and you have not. They can strike you down before you can deal with them."

The Amazon was silent. She knew Abna spoke the truth. Four-dimensional science was an art the Atlanteans thoroughly understood.

"Of course," Abna added, with a reassuring smile, "you have synthesis, and that is a secret we have yet to master."

The Amazon flashed a glance at him. "You don't intend to let me forget that, do you?"

"No reason why I should, is there? I was merely intimating that with synthesis you could put legions of zombies against me and create them as fast as I could destroy them. You might even beat me that way, by sheer weight of numbers."

The Amazon smiled faintly. "As for your race mastering synthesis, you will never learn that secret from me. I haven't forgotten that was one of the reasons you tried to trick me into marriage the last time."

Abna tightened his lips. "There was no trickery intended. The only trickery came from you, when you ran out on me on Mercury!"

There was a grim, smouldering silence for a moment; then Sefner Quorne came forward quietly. For the first time he spoke, in a richly mellow voice. "Perhaps, highness, this is an opportune moment to suggest a little refreshment for Miss Brant?"

Abna said, "Yes, excellency. See to it, will you?" The adviser withdrew and Abna continued:

"Have a seat, Vi. Let me have your suit."

She hesitated and then unfastened the clamps that caused the rubber-and-metal sheathing to fall away from her in slack folds. Abna took it and laid it on one side, following her thereafter to the table.

"Now," he said, seating himself comfortably, "let's talk like civilized people. You're far too nice a girl to be spitting brimstone with every word you utter."

The Amazon half opened her mouth to say something and then thought better of it.

Before Abna could speak again, the adviser returned, motioning to two servants to lay out the meal. When he was satisfied that everything was as it should be, he retired to a distance and remained watchful.

"I'm not particularly impressed by your adviser," the Amazon commented.

"Quorne?" Abna smiled a little. "Oh, he's all right, Vi. A bit tight-lipped but extremely efficient. I don't know what I'd do without him."

He began the task of serving the rich, exquisitely cooked food. "The issue," he said, when the meal was under way, "is quite simple, Vi. Either you marry me, or I shall have to perform the painful task of obliterating these Earth people whom you cherish so much."

She stared at him for a moment and then went on

eating as she thought the statement over. "How do you mean, obliterate them?" she questioned.

"You have seen the sixteen mirrors which ring this space-globe? They are so devised that they can bring the sun's rays into one focus from sixteen different points. Imagine those sixteen reflected rays concentrated into a single burning beam! A whole city could be destroyed in a matter of minutes by concentrated sunlight. It is just the little boy with the magnifying glass on a gigantic, scientific scale."

"So that is your intention!" Anger flamed again in the girl's eyes. "You would destroy the cities of Earth and resurrect Atlantis with its scientific devices, thereby enforcing a victory for yourself."

"That is my aim—and why not?" Abna shrugged. "It's so perfectly logical and therefore should appeal to you. I am still an Earthman at heart, remember, even though I was born on Jupiter. The Atlanteans were Earth people to begin with. I am merely intending to return to the world whence my race sprang. I know that as long as you rule the people of Earth, you will never submit to my control; so the only alternative is to destroy you—or them. I have too much regard for you to ever kill you, so the other way is to leave you with nobody to control, which means obliteration of Earth people, or else complete bondage."

"I'll stop you somehow."

"On the other hand," he continued, "you have a way out. Compromise by marrying me. Then, together, pooling our respective sciences, we can rule not only the Earth but my own small territory on Jupiter as well. You will add another world to your collection of colonised planets and everybody will be happy."

"The gain being all to you! You have no real love for me, Abna, even though I was once fool enough to think so. You simply regard me as a woman, and believe thereby that you can bring life once again to your dying race. You believe our offspring could form the basis of a new race."

"Mighty in strength and in knowledge," Abna agreed, smiling again. "What is so outlandish about that? We understand each other and can regard the biological implications dispassionately. I admit that is the primary reason for my desiring union with you, but it's not the only reason. I do love you, Vi, and always shall, even if we have to become sworn enemies through our differing viewpoints. A man who did not love you would never have gone through what I have to keep in contact with you. I would never have sought you out again after that synthesis trick you played on me. In the end, all universal issues come down to that one inescapable factor."

The Amazon relaxed, her lips tight. In her earlier contact with Abna, she had at times had to fight a similar battle to this, but never before had she so clearly realized that she had two sides to her fantastic character. The hard, cruel shell of a scientific woman which had gained her such tremendous power and eminence was at last desperately at war with the underlying woman, the woman who would not admit, even to herself, that she was becoming weary of her lone path, even a little nauseated at having greater power and intelligence than anybody else on Earth. The one side of her loathed the quiet mastery of Abna of Atlantis; the other side felt a sense of relief that a stronger personality could support her in moments when she was unsure.

"Naturally," Abna said, "it takes some thinking out—even though I should have imagined that you'd had time enough to consider in these past months. You knew perfectly well that I would return one day, and that union between us is inevitable in the end."

"I know nothing of the sort," she responded, without looking at him.

"It is inevitable because there is no room in the immediate solar system for both our sciences—and because we have too much regard for one another to resolve matters by destroying each other. If you have any doubts that I mean what I say, just come and watch this little episode."

Her meal finished, the Amazon rose and followed him across the control room until they reached an outlook port. Here Earth was in full view, greatly magnified by the lens of which the window itself was composed.

"There," Abna said, "is the United States. You recognize the outline? And there is England and Federation Europe. That greyness is the Atlantic and the darker grey running across it is newly risen Mu. If it were daylight instead of moonlight you'd see it more clearly. However, it is sufficient for our purpose."

"What purpose?" the Amazon asked in suspicion.

Abna summoned the adviser. He came forward like a ghost.

"Plan 19," Abna told him. "Proceed with it."

Sefner Quorne withdrew and moved over to the men still at the control board. He gave them instructions and then stood watching proceedings, alert for the slightest mistake. The Amazon gave a start as from the floating globe there stabbed a deep, lavender-coloured beam which lost itself in distance as it reached down toward Earth.

"What have you done?" she demanded flashing a glance at Abna's intently watching face. "Set fire to a city?"

"No, we have— There! See?"

The girl looked at a brief flash of flame. Then the lavender beam faded out and the hum of power from the atomic plant ceased.

"Satisfactory, highness?" Sefner Quorne inquired.

"Entirely," Abna assented, and to the Amazon he added, "I have destroyed the force-dome existing round Atlantis. That is the first move. I shall next travel to Atlantis and resurrect its scientific weapons. I must go quickly before your Earthly curiosity-mongers start investigating. After that will come the destruction of every city, unless we compromise."

The girl made a bewildered movement. "Abna, I do not understand you!" she declared. "Whatever I may think of you, I have never considered you a man of violence. I honestly do not believe that you would deliberately kill a whole race of people just to get me. You haven't the necessary ruthlessness for that!"

"You underrate me," he replied. "There was a time in the past when you killed thousands to try to master the world: why shouldn't I perform a similar action for, to me—a far greater prize—to get you?"

The Amazon said nothing and Abna's reddish eyes regarded her steadily. "One word from you can stop it all, Vi. However," he added, smiling, "think it over. I shall not go to Earth to deal with Atlantis until tomorrow. In the meantime you are my guest. Excellency!"

Sefner Quorne came over without a sound.

Abna said: "Please see that Miss Brant has the guest suite. And you'll forgive me, Vi," he added to her, "if I place a guard outside your door. With you right here in my hands I would be a fool indeed if I gave you any opportunity to escape!"

CHAPTER THREE
DUEL IN SPACE

Aboard the London-New York airliner Ethel Wilson sat gazing intently into the night. The liner was two hours late in departing, a delay occasioned by a changing of route due to atmospheric upheavals still present after the arrival of the land-strip across the Atlantic.

Now Ethel sat in the observation room and solarium in the tail of the liner, a glass-walled section for passengers who wished to enjoy the view. The glass was specially treated so that it screened out harmful radiation. She was alone in the dim light, carefully arranged so that it gave no reflection from the glass floor, roof, and walls.

Having made clear the purpose of her journey, and her identity being well known, it had not been difficult to have the commander arrange for twin flood beams to illuminate the course below. In consequence the rocky terrain where there had once been ocean now lay bright as day to Ethel's searching gaze.

A tremendous concussion struck the airliner. It flung Ethel out of her seat and she slithered helplessly across the glass floor, colliding with the wall. The liner tipped alarmingly, nose down, out of control. Unable to get on her feet, Ethel lay staring through the glass floor, dazzled by a bewildering amethyst brilliance bathing the liner. To her ears came the scream of the wind outside and, from within the great craft, the ringing of alarm bells and the desperate shouts of people.

There was not time to escape. The machine was not high enough to allow it. With the pale purple light still coruscating around it, it hit the rocks below with thunderous impact.

Ethel found herself still alive and conscious, though dazed. The walls and floor of the glass room were crumpled into powder, the glass being incapable of splintering.

Her shoulders bruised and her head aching, Ethel dragged herself to her feet and clawed her way through the broken framework of the window, so reaching the rocks outside. Looking about her, she realized that the glass observation room with its absence of solid metal supports and girders had saved her life. The remainder of the liner had crashed nose-first and completely telescoped, fire blazing from it. What had happened to the passengers Ethel did not know, but apparently only a few had survived.

She turned away, getting as far as possible from the wreck in case it blew up—not from liquid fuel, since it did not use that for motive power, but from the fusing of the atom plant. When she had moved perhaps half a mile, there was a shattering concussion behind her, the back-draught of wind nearly blowing her from her feet. She looked back at a slowly subsiding cascade of sparks, then the pale moonlight was the only illumination left.

"Pretty grim, isn't it?" a voice asked behind her, and she whirled round. In the moonlight a heavily built man in tattered pilot's uniform came toward her, his dark hair dishevelled.

"You're a survivor?" Ethel asked him.

"Yes. About a dozen got away. I'm First Pilot Barry Schofield."

Ethel asked: "Have you any idea what happened?"

"Something completely abnormal. Nearest way I can explain it is to say it was like a very prolonged flash of lightning. We stood no chance against it. Climatic upheaval to blame, I suppose."

"I suppose so," Ethel agreed.

"Are you hurt, Miss—?"

"No; thanks all the same. Just shaken, that's all. The name is Wilson."

"You mean Ethel Wilson?" the pilot asked in surprise. "Quite an honour, Miss Wilson. I've heard of you, of course, the daughter of Mr. Wilson of the Dodd Space Line."

Ethel said no more just then. She could dimly see the pilot looking about him upon the rocky moonlit terrain. Presently he gave a rather ironical laugh.

"I suppose we should be thankful for this mysterious plateau which has been born, otherwise we might have plunged into the sea, which would certainly have put paid to everybody. The puzzle now is which way to go. The last bearings we took showed we were about halfway between America and Europe." He looked up at the stars. "In that case we now have our backs to England, so I suppose we'd better start moving. There wasn't time to send a radio message, but when we fail to turn up in the United States there'll be search parties flying over to look for us. In the meantime, walking will keep the chill out of our bones."

"We might do better if we headed for Atlantis," Ethel said, thinking. "Or would we? No, perhaps not, since it's covered with a dome of some sort."

"Did you say Atlantis?" the pilot asked in surprise.

"Yes. At least my aunt, Miss Brant, thinks it might be that city in the middle of this plateau. It can't be far from here. Not that it matters, though, because the dome over it will prevent us getting any shelter."

The pilot said, "You may find these rocks slippery, and a broken ankle or leg would be no joke at a time like this."

"How right you are," Ethel agreed.

* * * * * * *

In her sumptuous suite aboard Abna's space-globe, and with the door securely locked and presumably guards on duty outside it, the Amazon stood for a while gazing out of the window upon Earth and turning over possible plans for escape.

The time had not yet come when she was willing to bow down to one man's orders. The woman in her was not so much uppermost that she let it swamp her scientific judgment. The time to talk would come, she believed, when she had proved she was Abna's equal— that she could beat him as he could beat her. Until then, she was determined to ignore his proposal, if she could.

Certainly she had got to escape somehow, and marshal her forces against whatever attack Abna decided upon. If she did not, her only way to save humanity would be to give way to the young giant which, however much it might appeal to her as woman, went utterly against the grain as a scientist.

As she gazed thoughtfully through the window she became aware that her *Ultra* was no more than fifteen feet distant outside, the nose firmly anchored to the spherical wall of the space-globe by the magnetism that was evidently passing through the outer plates. She considered this fact and then passed her fingers along the belt about her waist, which Abna had not taken from her.

Walking beside the wall of her suite, she measured it as closely as possible and judged that the *Ultra*'s nose was affixed to the outside of this very wall, in a remote corner.

She pondered for several minutes, weighing up the scientific implications and her power of physical resistance. The problem was if she could get into space— as she knew she could by cutting the wall open with the protonic gun she had in her belt, working on the narrowest beam—could she survive the deadly void and airlessness long enough to reach the safety lock of her machine and get inside?

"Yes, I can," she told herself, finally. "A body in outer space only explodes if it is full of air. There being no pressure outside it just flies apart. If I expel all the air from my lungs as I plunge I should do it. As for space, it is a perfect insulator of heat: I shall radiate warmth faster than it can escape, so the absence of temperature will make no impression on me."

Her decision made, she took the protonic gun from the holster on her belt and adjusted the nozzle so that a hair-thin pencil of destructive energy would jet from the instrument when she pressed the switch. She spent a further few minutes weighing up the approximate position of the *Ultra* attached to the spherical wall outside, and then went to work, narrowing her eyes before the brightness of the blue-white fire that bit into the metal.

The metal sizzled, tough though it was, and then began to flow as its atomic makeup collapsed. As the Amazon well knew the moment a fissure to the exterior was created the air would whistle out of this suite. Her task was to see that it did not expend itself gradually but in one complete explosion, the force of which would blow the *Ultra* clear and, the magnetism of the plating destroyed once a circle was cut out, the *Ultra* would be released.

So, working with great care, she traced a deep circular line, which approximately encompassed the *Ultra*'s nose. She was calculating that a blow on the bitten metal would drive the rough circle clean out into the void, when a sound made her swing round.

A guard came in, a suspicious look on his dour face. He stared for a moment at the Amazon holstering her proton-gun, then at the circle she had traced in the wall. He seemed slow to grasp her intentions, but the moment he did so he turned back to the door, presumably with the intention of calling Abna.

Before he reached the door, the Amazon sprang lithely and slammed it, her back to it. The guard stopped, hand on his gun.

"I would much prefer, my friend, that you do not sound the alarm," she explained. "I realise that you are under orders and obeying them: for that reason I shan't harm you if you remain passive. Otherwise...," and she clenched her fingers at her sides.

The guard seemed in two minds as to his course of action; then he realised his hand was on his gun. He whipped it out of his holster. Whether he intended to fire it or use it as a threat the Amazon did not know. Rather than take a chance she lashed out her right fist with the speed of uncoiling spring. Back of it was the superhuman strength of her muscles.

The guard took the blow on the jaw, his head snapped back as if on a hinge, and he went flying helplessly across the room. Entirely by chance he collided with the carved section of metal in the wall and the impact jarred it outward with a violent crack. Instantly the air in the suite gushed outward n a mighty blast.

Helplessly the Amazon was torn across the room and flung out into space with the unconscious—perhaps dead—guard somersaulting ahead of her. She had the presence of mind to expel every vestige of air from her lungs, then with all her strength she jackknifed her legs up and down in a kicking motion, as in swimming, to force herself upward to the looming bulk of the *Ultra*.

Her hands struck the metalwork of the *Ultra* and she whirled herself up with superlative ease, the gravity being practically nonexistent. In floating leaps she gained the safety-lock on top of the vessel, snapped back the cover, and dropped below. In a few moments she was through the second doorway and half fell into the control room, gulping for breath as normal air was around her once more.

Red-faced, her heart banging like a trip-hammer, she fell in the control chair and gradually forced herself to normal again. Then she peered outside. As she had calculated, the *Ultra* was free of the space-globe, the circular piece of rent metal floating in the void, chained between the attraction of the *Ultra* and the globe. Afar off, incredibly bloated and in parts torn, was the dead body of the guard.

The Amazon swung the *Ultra* away, but when in a moment or two she had gone ten miles, she slowed down again, thinking. There were perhaps other possibilities about her escape of which she had not taken account. Had all the air escaped from the space-globe through the hole she had made? If so, not a soul aboard would be alive, not even Abna. She did not know why this caused her sudden anxiety, but it did. After all, she was his enemy. She had risked death to escape him and yet—

"Congratulations, Vi!" a voice exclaimed abruptly through the ever-open radio receiver and she gave a start and a half sigh of relief as she recognized the voice of Abna. "Apparently you'll take any chance," he continued, "but I don't think it will do you any good. I'm going to have you brought back right now! If you planned to let all the air out of this globe you weren't successful. Every room is hermetically sealed off with its own air supply, so we're none of us hurt."

The Amazon snapped on the microphone. "You're not going to bring me back, Abna. Since you've chosen to fight me I'm going to fight back with everything I've got."

She set the *Ultra* moving towards the mighty sphere, gathering speed as fast as she could in so short a distance. She had discovered that the globe hung in space because it was poised between the gravitational fields of Earth and Moon, following an orbit like a satellite. One thrust either way would be sufficient to unbalance it for many hours until the critical field was found again.

Faster the *Ultra* travelled as the Amazon thought on these things, and faster still. If magnetism were hurled to her now she could avoid it by driving the *Ultra* through the hole in the sphere; but the chances were that the magnetism was short-circuited by the hole, the plates being discontinuous. Indeed, this did seem to be the answer, for as she hurtled nearer to the globe there was nothing on her instruments to show that magnetism was at work.

Then she hit the sphere with the impact of a battering ram. Doubtless it dented the *Ultra*'s armoured nose, but the force was not sufficient to crack it. She felt the springs of the control seat crack as she was pressed back with the shock. Promptly she reversed the power plant, causing the *Ultra* to slow down and then move in the opposite direction.

Through the windows she watched the huge globe rolling over and over, ponderously thrown completely off balance and moving away from her, plunging off the deadline into the grip of the Moon. With a chuckle she switched on the microphone.

"Think that one over, Abna!" she cried. "You can save yourself, but in the time it takes you to get that football of yours balanced up again I'll get back to Earth and have a look at Atlantis for myself."

There was no response, possibly because things inside the globe were in hopeless confusion. Still smiling triumphantly, the Amazon switched off, swung round the *Ultra*'s nose, and darted with ever-increasing speed toward the Earth twenty thousand miles below.

CHAPTER FOUR
MONSTERS

It was dawn when the Amazon found herself nosing the *Ultra* down into the stratosphere. Automatically the speed slowed under the drag of ever-deepening atmosphere. Watching intently through the forward port, she found herself descending over Canada. Within a few moments she had set the course right and streaked at thousands of miles an hour to the southeast for the newly risen land of Mu in the Atlantic Ocean.

As she travelled she made a meal of essences and tablets, more than sufficient to restore her strength; then an hour later the rolling waters of the Atlantic gave place to the rocky shores of the newborn continent and her speed diminished again. She cruised the *Ultra* at a mere 150 miles an hour at a height of 2,000 feet, watching intently for the first sign of Atlantis.

Long before the city itself loomed in view, she was astonished to behold something else—life, incredible life. Roaming about the vast plateau, life of a kind not seen on Earth since the days of the Mesozoic era. In the space of a few minutes she identified the grey, huge shapes moving below as the Atlantosaurus,

Brontosaurus, and Diplodocus. They moved with the slow ponderousness of tanks, searching endlessly for food, utterly lost in this rocky waste and belonging to an age long gone.

As she gazed, the *Ultra* suddenly jolted from the impact of something flying through the air. She looked upwards in amazement, in time to see the unmistakable shape of a flying lizard, a pterodactyl, sweeping off with the speed of a hawk into the dawn sky.

"Of course," she whispered at last, as she considered the problem. "That force dome covering Atlantis must have preserved everything within it in a kind of perpetual stasis—including living creatures! Those monsters must have been preserved under the dome for thousands of years, and now, with the breaking of the dome, they've revived and are escaping to the outer world!" A frown creased her forehead. "But how were they existing at the time of Atlantis? They should have been extinct millions of years earlier...."

The solution to the mystery would have to wait. For now, between Europe and America, there was a strip of dry land, along which the monsters could move. It would only be a question of time before they found their way to civilisation, and then— She sat dumbly for a moment, appalled at the prospect of these monstrous beasts turned loose in London or New York.

The *Ultra* flew onward as she pondered. She passed over a herd of mastodons, colossal elephants with curved, ground-length tusks. Not far behind them, roaming in rocks in partly upright postures, came cave bears three times the size of any normal bear. The thought oppressed her now that she must warn both London and New York of what might happen if these ravenous beasts travelled that far.

She raised her eyes to look again for Atlantis and saw it now on the distant horizon, free of the dome that had formerly covered it; but there was something even more surprising—two lone figures, a man and woman, much the worse for wear, making their way amidst the rocks. As the *Ultra* flew above them, the Amazon saw them frantically waving to attract her attention. She slowed speed and came back in a circle. Flying again over the two, she realized who the woman was.

"Ethel!" she exclaimed blankly and brought the flier down gently to the rocks perhaps half a mile from Ethel and the young pilot staggering along with her.

Opening the airlock, the Amazon stepped out to the rocky plateau and began to advance toward the pair coming toward her. Then she gave a shout of warning. Out of the empty spaces a mighty shape with corrugated back was looming, the dawn sunlight glinting on his armoured sides. He had evidently been hidden by the rocks. He was at least eighty feet long and thirty feet high, a perfect specimen of the Ceratosaurus.

"Run!" the Amazon shouted, pulling out her proton gun. "Look what's behind you!"

In turning to glance, the young man caught his foot in a rock crevice and went sprawling. Ethel got ahead of him by a few yards and then swung around in horror, staring up at the colossal beast racing forward. The young man made an effort to get up, convinced as he did so that a mighty foot would descend upon him with obliterating impact. The Amazon stopped, sighted her proton gun and pressed the button. It was still on the smallest nozzle and from it there jetted a hair-thin line of disintegrative fire. She aimed for the ridged eyes of the colossus. It reared with a shriek, lashing around a vast tail that missed the pilot by inches. He lay crouching, afraid to run in case he made his position worse.

Again the Amazon fired and the biting vibration struck right through to the creature's vitals. He gave one last howl of anguish, slewed around, then dropped.

"Aunt Vi—!"

Her name being screamed by Ethel whirled the Amazon around. She saw Ethel standing paralyzed with fear, looking into the eyes of a terrifying beast perched on top of a nearby rock. It was flawlessly striped, crouching for the spring, wide green eyes staring with baleful fixity. From the upper jaw, two enormous fanged teeth projected. The Amazon had time to realize the creature was the huge sabre-toothed tiger of bygone days—then it sprang.

The Amazon sprang simultaneously, delivering a blow at Ethel that knocked her spinning half a dozen yards to collapse half-conscious in the rocks. The impact knocked the Amazon's gun out of her hand, and simultaneously the tiger knocked her backwards to the stony ground.

Within a matter of seconds the big, savagely strong

beast was snarling beside her, the upper lips drawn back over the merciless fangs. Those few seconds gave her just time to fling up her hands to save herself. Instantly her fingers were buried in the glossy throat. She crushed fiercely, squeezing with every scrap of her strength, keeping the devilish face a foot away from her own.

Straining every muscle, she fought her way up from a lying position and gradually edged up her left knee until it was under the tiger. She kicked and flung her hands forward simultaneously, winding the beast and shifting him a couple of feet away. With this split second advantage she got to her feet. Ethel, the young pilot beside her, was searching frantically for the fallen proton gun.

The Amazon backed, keeping her eyes on the creature, watching it flatten for the spring. It came, a hurtling, living battering ram. She braced herself for it and this time deliberately thrust her right hand in the beast's mouth, using a knee as a brace against its spine. In those seconds she had it at her mercy. Her knee pressed into the spine and her hand dragged down with ever-tightening force on the beast's lower jaw, making it impossible for it to close its deadly mouth. With it thrashing helplessly against her body, the Amazon dragged and strained harder and harder and presently brought her left hand into play as well. Lower she pulled and lower, until she heard and felt the jaw hinge snap and the wounded beast scream with pain. It lashed mightily with its claws, but to no purpose since they only struck air.

The Amazon held on, her hands moving to the creature's neck. Then she slid her forearms in position and locked them about the throat, bending the broad back against her leg. She sank on one knee, leaving the other knee to act as a bridge. The result was inevitable. The ever-increasing pressure finally snapped the spine of the beast and it sagged, eyes glazing.

Breathing stormily from her exertions, the Amazon reeled on her feet again and moved unsteadily. Slowly Ethel and the young man moved toward her, Ethel holding out the proton gun she had at last located.

"Thanks," the Amazon acknowledged, tucking it in its holster. "I could have done with it a lot sooner—if both of you had not been so scared!"

The young man winced at the contemptuous look in the Amazon's violet eyes, but not so Ethel.

"All very well for you to talk, Aunt Vi! You don't expect us to behave as you do surely?"

"Forget it." The Amazon glanced about the rocky terrain, to find it peaceful for the moment. Turning back to Ethel, she asked a question: "What on earth are you doing here?"

Ethel gave the details and introduced Barry Schofield. He smiled rather awkwardly as he shook the Amazon's yellow hand.

"I suppose it sounds a bit silly to say I'm honoured to meet you, Miss Brant? But I am, you know! It really means something to be introduced to the Golden Amazon."

The Amazon surveyed him in her aloof fashion and then gave a shrug.

"I'm glad you were present, Mr. Schofield, to look after my niece. What I have to do now is get the pair of you back to London before worse things befall us. It's extremely fortunate I decided to come this way to have a look at Atlantis."

"You're still going to explore it, of course?" Ethel asked eagerly.

"In which you wish to join me?" The Amazon shook her head. "I'm not exploring it now—later, perhaps. There's going to be a good deal of trouble in London with these prehistoric monsters, and I feel I should be present to deal with them. America, too, must be warned."

The two young people went ahead of her to the *Ultra* and she set the machine climbing. Presently she turned and glanced at Barry Schofield.

"Are you accustomed to flying a fighter plane, Mr. Schofield?"

He nodded. "I can fly anything, Miss Brant, probably even this machine of yours."

"That is an opportunity I do not propose to grant you," the Amazon answered and sized him up with her disconcertingly steady look.

He was not aware of it, but in those few moments his thoughts had been read and his character determined. The effort of thought-reading was one the Amazon rarely made, and she only did it now because she as reasonably sure that Ethel found the young man attractive. Certainly he was good-natured in expression, with a somewhat impudent nose, a friendly grin, black hair, and grey eyes.

"Will you want me to fly a fighter?" he asked, and the Amazon nodded. She moved her gaze to Ethel.

"You as well, Ethel. Every man and woman who can fly will be needed, and their job will be to hunt down these monsters and destroy them."

She turned back to the controls and Ethel began to prepare a meal. When she had it laid on the control table, she moved to the Amazon's side and spoke in a low voice. "Aunt Vi, you read his thoughts, didn't you?" she whispered. "I could tell by your expression. Is he the sort of man he seems? I mean, do you approve?"

The Amazon gave one of her rare, genuine smiles, and it transformed the frigid beauty of her face into momentary gentleness. "I approve entirely," she murmured. "Quite a clean-living, clean-minded young man."

Ethel smiled and withdrew. At the silent Barry Schofield, who was plainly wondering what was going on, she merely gave a glance. Reserve kept her from saying just then what she thought. She was content for the moment to let friendship develop along normal channels.

* * * * * * *

By the time the meal was over, the shores of Britain were visible as a smudge on the distant skyline and as yet, no monsters had been sighted as having reached this far. The last herd of them was now some twenty miles to the rear but this only applied to the land juggernauts. As the *Ultra* came ever closer to London, it was obvious that high over the city there circled the winged lizard forms of pterodactyls, apparently ravenous and yet bewildered by the city.

Twenty minutes more brought the *Ultra* to the heart of London, to the roof of the building that formed her home and executive headquarters. It was only a matter of a few moments before she, Ethel, and Barry were in the main offices where a worried Chris Wilson immediately seized his daughter in his arms and kissed her fervently.

He whispered, stroking her dark hair, "I got the news from New York that your liner had never arrived and as the hours passed I—"

"Sorry to interrupt, Chris, but this is no time for sentiment," the Amazon interjected. "There's trouble heading this way and I just wish to stay long enough to give you some orders to carry out, then I'm hurrying back to Atlantis—to meet trouble of another sort from Abna."

She gave the details briefly as Chris looked at her in surprise; then his expression changed.

"Prehistoric monsters? Coming here? Is—is that what those things are flying in the sky?"

"They're pterodactyls," the Amazon explained. "What did you think they were?"

"I don't quite know—or care. I was so worried about Ethel, nothing else seemed to matter."

"Then it's time we got to business," the Amazon said, sitting at the communications desk. "This young man is Barry Schofield. I've told you how he helped Ethel along."

Chris shook hands warmly with the young pilot, and in the midst of exchanging conversations, the Amazon remained at the microphone and spoke deliberately.

"Relay this announcement from all public speakers. All men and women who can fly a fighter plane are to report immediately to the Central Airport for instructions."

She changed the switch to the airport itself and spoke to the chief executive.

"Liner 79-2 crashed last night on its way to New York and there may be survivors. Send rescue planes to search and have them heavily armed with atomic guns. Wherever prehistoric monsters are seen they must be destroyed. Repeat—prehistoric monsters. That is not a misstatement. You will also order all fighter plane commanders to have their fleets gather in and around the central airport. Skilled and unskilled pilots will fly those planes between here and the United States, destroying every prehistoric monster they can find. Inform the American authorities of our intentions and have them do likewise."

The Amazon switched off and relaxed a little, then she rose from the desk to contemplate the trio facing her.

"You, Ethel and you, Mr. Schofield—or maybe I'd netter call you Barry from here on—will take off in fighter planes the moment you are rested. Later, if Abna does what I think he will, you may have to do battle with whatever power he unleashes from Atlantis, unless I get there first and pull the props from under him."

"You mean you couldn't come to any compromise with him?" Chris asked.

"I could, but I wouldn't. His ultimatum—if you can call it such—is the same as before. Marriage, or destruction of the Earth race. I intend to show him that I can give as good as he sends."

"But, Aunt Vi," Ethel exclaimed, "are you sure that's the right course? After all, as I've said before, as we've all pointed out—"

The Amazon gestured impatiently. "I've made my choice," she interrupted. "There's nothing more to be discussed. Now I must be on my way to Atlantis before Abna gets—"

The remainder of her words were drowned by a thunderous crash from the windows. The entire frame came hurtling inward as a mighty horned beak struck it. A flying, leathery horror, panic-stricken by its chance collision with the glass, came flapping ponderously into the great office, its horned and socketed eyes gleaming with the evil intentness of a snake.

"A pterodactyl!" Chris yelled, and with one mighty effort seized Ethel and hurled her under the broad centre desk. In a matter of seconds he had followed her.

The Amazon was not so lucky. She tried to wrench

out her gun but at the same instant the blindly flying horror clamped its fanged beak about her waist and lifted her into the air. Only one thing saved her from being bitten in twain by those scissor-sharp jaws, and that was the hard gold of her instrument belt.

She did not attempt to move, knowing only too well that this might shift her body into the danger line. At the moment the yellow fangs were biting hard and uselessly into the gold as the monster still flew wildly around the office, trying to find the window through which it had accidentally come.

Chris picked up a heavy desk chair, waiting for a chance to land a blow; then he paused as Barry aimed him a quick glance.

"Take it easy, Mr. Wilson," he said. "I'll get the brute."

He dashed across to the tall record cabinet and stood on it; then as the pterodactyl came hurtling toward him, the Amazon lying limply in its jaws, the young pilot sprang upward with all his strength and clutched hold of one of the enormous webbed feet, hanging on to it desperately as he swayed and tossed about the office.

"Your proton gun," he panted, the Amazon's face a couple of feet above him. "Which holster?"

She bent an arm and pointed to the holster in question, her angle such that she could not reach it herself. Barry struggled higher, never once releasing his grip of the mighty flying lizard as it tried to shake him off.

Finally, holding with one hand, he reached up with the other and yanked the gun free; then he let himself drop to the office floor. Crouching he aimed the gun carefully as the thing circled. It seemed that by now it had discovered where lay the smashed window, but before it could reach it and take the Amazon with it, needle-pointed fire stabbed into the underside of the lizard.

With the shriek it gave, it opened its jaws wide and the Amazon fell free, crashing to the desk and sliding from it to the floor. Dazed, she collapsed in a corner. Barry remained where he was, firing again.

Already dying, the monster flapped helplessly toward the window; then suddenly one of its shattered wings gave way and it toppled over in mid-air to go sailing down into the street below and drop dead.

"That was wonderful!" Ethel cried, catching his arm.

The Amazon rose and came over, taking the gun from his hand and holstering it.

"I had thought of you as not over-courageous, Barry," she said. "Now I know differently." She gave Ethel a meaning look and then added: "You can also see the kind of trouble we're up against with these monsters. Better get busy as soon as you can and clean them up. I'll dispose of as many as possible on my way to Atlantis."

She turned and went quickly from the office, laving Ethel and Barry staring after her. The pilot scratched his head.

"She came that near to death and doesn't even blink an eyelash about it," he declared. "Damned if I can understand it!"

"You will, son," Chris assured him drily. "And consider yourself complimented! For the Amazon to praise anybody is a phenomenon! She's never praised me once in all the years I've known her."

CHAPTER FIVE
QUORNE STRIKES

On her journey back to Atlantis across the plateau, the Amazon singled out and destroyed eight of the massive land beasts and could have killed more had not time been so pressing.

It was mid-morning when she brought the *Ultra* down close to the newly risen city, and for a moment or two she sat in the control seat, surveying. Apparently Abna had not yet made good his intention to come to the city, unless he was concealed somewhere within it, knowing that eventually she would come to explore. This, however, was a chance she was prepared to take.

The city had the beauty of an ancient but superb architecture. Minarets and domes, apparently gold-tipped and glinting in the bright sunlight, seemed to be the predominant feature. The edifices were of white stone preserved through the centuries reaching down to well-laid streets. Graceful trees, which bespoke the fact that once this region had been tropical, were swaying in the wind, in as good condition as on the day the dome had been clamped over them.

The Amazon took out her proton gun, recharged it

with a rack of cheap diamonds from which the power was derived; then with it in her hand she opened the airlock and stepped out into the sunlight. She walked down the main street, surveying window frames in which there was no glass, pausing to look into large rooms tastefully furnished in Oriental style and as flawlessly preserved as everything else.

She began to appreciate after a while that here in this main street were all the living quarters, ranging from the sumptuous halls of the one-time dignitaries to the smaller dwellings of the less important. Whatever scientific equipment there was must be housed in other parts of the town. An hour of wandering down the well-laid main streets, their floors patterned in exquisite mosaic with gold inlays and climbing up and down terraces so designed that each one gave an overall view of the city, brought her to the region she sought. Here, in mighty halls, silent now but expressive of the vast industry that had at one time been prevalent.

She found great power plants and laboratories that bore the stamp of superb science long deserted and forgotten.

In one laboratory she thought she recognized machines that would have meaning for her. She drew herself over the low window ledge and began to walk down the aisle between the silent mechanical giants.

There were generators, tremendous turbines which seemed to have an atomic basis, whole banks of transformers, multiple switchboards—a vision of power which was frightening when she came to think of it as applied against her own resources which, though by no means negligible, were meagre, because since the Glacier onslaught she had not had time to build up any formidable array of weapons—or indeed had she ever imagined there would be any immediate need of them.

A sound made her turn sharply and for a moment she could not quite believe what she saw. Looking at her around the rim of a dynamo was a face. In the bright sunlight it seemed reddish. She gazed fixedly upon lank dark hair hanging over a low, receding brow. The eyes, deep reddish-brown, were watching her in fascination, from under beetling brows. The cheekbones were high, the nose broad and flat at the base, the mouth projecting in the fashion of an ape.

"Java man," the Amazon breathed, astounded. "*Pithecanthropus erectus*, one of the earliest forms of man! This is utterly fantastic! These creatures walked the Earth more than 500,000 years ago, millions of years *after* dinosaurs died out and thousands of years *before* Atlantis. And yet, he was coexisting with the monsters when he was trapped under the dome and came alive again—now."

Suddenly he came from his hiding place into full view—a creature naked save for the crude skin loincloth in which lay a stone-hilted dagger. His chest and shoulders were vastly developed and muscular, his arms so long that the knuckles touched the floor as he moved. In height he stood perhaps five feet six.

He sprang, with one mighty leaping movement of his iron-muscled legs. The Amazon depressed the gun button, but to her horror the first crude diamond charge locked in its detonator case and no protonic beam came forth. The heavy hairy body cannoned straight at her, knocking her from her feet.

Instantly, she flung up her hands to protect herself, seizing the thick sinewy neck—but here was a creature with strength equalling and indeed surpassing her own. His powerful hands seized her arms and flattened them hard on the mosaic floor. One massive knee planted itself perhaps an inch from her throat. The creature looked at her dumbly, uttering no words, but breathing hard and grumbling to himself after the fashion of an ape.

Fear was usually unknown to the Amazon, but this time she did feel its sharp barb. She had only one weapon left—hypnosis. With an effort she brought her gaze into focus and stared relentlessly and unblinkingly into the reddish orbs. As she did so, she moved her legs gently upward in readiness for a scissoring, thrusting movement.

But staring into those intense violet eyes filled with battering intelligence from a highly developed brain did not seem to have much effect on the creature.

She did the only other thing possible. Doubling her legs to the limit, she rammed up her knees violently, striking the apeman in the stomach. He gasped and choked at the unexpected blow and his grip relaxed.

Instantly the Amazon was on her feet and struck him with the gun on the side of the head, and he gave a yelp. A split second later he lashed out a blow with his right fist; unable to judge the abnormal length of his arm, the Amazon took the blow in the face and staggered back, coming up hard against a machine. Then the apeman pushed her against the metalwork, his strong hands forcing her arms back so that she could not do any more damage.

She writhed and struggled desperately to free herself. She felt her back must break between the pressure of his body and the metal rim of the machine. Then suddenly he had gone from her. She was too dazed for a moment to understand why. Bruised, gasping for breath, she winced as she straightened up, then amazement banished some of her pain and fear.

The apeman had not released her of his own accord. He had been forced to do so. A big figure in a golden, one-piece costume had appeared and had a mighty arm about the apeman's throat, forcing him backward to the floor—but only for a moment. The apeman tore free and whirled to do battle with his stone knife. The golden-suited giant was ready. His hand shot out and gripped the long arm by the wrist, forcing it backward with remorseless pressure.

The left hand came around a second later and gripped the apeman by the throat, forcing him to his knees. Knowing the great strength of the apeman, the Amazon could only watch in awe at the even greater strength of the newcomer. The stone knife went flying.

The giant's fist slammed into the apeman's face, battering him back on to the floor, and the creature began to shriek and finally tried to turn tail.

The golden-suited man caught the creature by the ankle, whirling him up and around over his head and then releasing him. He flew helplessly in a dizzy arc and struck the metal stanchion of a machine. His skull smashed, he collapsed with a thump to the mosaic floor and lay still.

The giant turned and the Amazon wondered why she had not known him from his height. She was unwilling to admit that she was too shaken and demoralized to grasp the situation at all at the moment.

"Apparently this is no place for girls," Abna commented, coming forward. "And apparently, you are not nearly so tough as you make out, Vi."

She stared at him in perplexity—even mortification.

"How did you get here?" she demanded. "I admit it was providential—but how did you find me?"

"Sure you're not hurt?" he asked.

"Answer my question! How did you get here?"

"Not very difficult. From the space-globe—once we got it on even keel again after you so kindly overbalanced us!—I turned the telescope on Atlantis to see what effect there was from the removal of the dome. The first thing I saw was your *Ultra* lying near it. With such a heaven-sent chance to get at you, I took it—and came."

The girl frowned. "You were incredibly rapid!"

Abna chuckled. "Surely I don't have to explain to you about instantaneous transportation? You've often used it, transferring a body in atomic form from place to place and reassembling the body at the point of arrival. You even explored Mars that way once. I used that method, chiefly because speed was essential. I saw the danger you might be in."

"How could you? You couldn't see inside this building, surely?"

"No, but I could see the prehistoric life roving about the plateau, so I thought you'd need protection. Apparently I was right, too."

The Amazon straightened up, completely recovered. She gave a cynical smile.

"Yes, I have to admit that 1 was caught off guard that time—but only because of my gun," she added defensively, and examining it, she pulled free the faulty diamond and replaced it with a new one. Then she put the gun back in its holster.

"And now you are here, Abna, what have you in mind?" she asked. "You wish to capture me, I suppose? If so, think again. My gun is in order now."

"I've only one wish, Vi, the same I've had all along—for you to marry me."

"Or else you'll destroy civilization and what there is in this city in the way of scientific devices?"

Abna said nothing for a moment and in the silence there rose the faint scream of fast travelling planes and the concussion of falling bombs.

"Fliers," the Amazon explained. "I detailed them to destroy these monsters wherever they can before they invade civilization. Probably you thought it was a clever idea to release prehistoric men and monsters to create panic? In a few hours they'll all be taken care of."

The Amazon frowned as a thought struck her. "I still can't reconcile the fact that creatures from widely separated geological eras could have been alive in the first place and existing in Atlantis."

Abna gave her a serious look. "In all honesty, Vi, I never knew those brutes and cavemen existed when the force dome was closed around Atlantis. However, I checked our historical records before leaving, and discovered that my ancestors had recreated different geological eras, and their life forms, as a scientific experiment to prove their theories on evolution. You'll remember that my ancestors had to evacuate in a hurry when cosmic disaster threatened. They barely had time to create the stasis dome to preserve and protect the city—"

"So they just left these creatures behind?"

"That's how it looks," Abna agreed. "And without anyone there when they revived, they've evidently escaped from their reservation areas. All of these creatures around us were the result of centuries of controlled mutations on animals of our own time which were devolved over successive generations until their earlier forms were recreated...."

"Including humans?" the Amazon snapped. "The whole concept of the experiment is utterly repulsive—"

Abna spread his hands. "I'm sorry, Vi, but I can't be held responsible for the actions of my ancestors any more than you can be for the Spanish Inquisition—but I can help you destroy the creatures, if need be."

"Help me?" the girl repeated. "Why should you? You have a potent panic-weapon there. A few monsters in a crowded city would very soon disrupt morale—"

"Listen, Vi!" Suddenly she found her shoulders gripped, Abna looking down into her face intently. "I don't expect you to believe this, but I'll have to admit it because I'm forced to. I haven't the least intention of destroying your civilisation, or of hurting anybody more than I can help. I raised Atlantis for only one purpose—because I knew that you would realize I was responsible for it and would seek out the cause. I knew also that you would hear of my space-globe from the space-liner pilots. You came out into space. I'd hoped then that you'd see reason, patch our quarrel, and marry me. I don't give a hoot about Atlantis, and I certainly don't want the trouble of reviving it for destruction—only for peaceful uses with you to help me as my queen. The people who were killed in the tidal wave were victims of bad calculations on my part, not deliberate murder. As with the monsters, it was something I overlooked. That's the truth, Vi. I swear it is!"

The Amazon said nothing. She was so astonished at his about-face that she suspected a trick somewhere. And yet....

* * * * * * *

Ethel Wilson sat at the control board of her little fighter plane, keenly watching the view below reflected through prismatic screens, her left hand on the button of the atomic-shell gun, her right on the single calibrated wheel which guided the fast machine. Around her were the five other fliers who had departed with her as squadron nine from the London airport on a 'monster' hunt. Not far away, first in the formation that spread to her left, she could see Barry Schofield's head behind the window of his cabin.

Ahead of this squadron eight others had already departed and as the approximate centre of the giant Murian plateau was reached, the squadron split up at an order from the commander, to begin the hunting of the beasts visible in the rocky wastes below. Others, much nearer to the British end of the land strip, were already being handled by another group of fighters.

Ethel began to enjoy herself, focusing the monstrous beasts in the hair-crossline of the gunsight and pressing the button. Not that she was vicious by nature, but she loved action and danger and the carefree sensation always produced by hurtling flying. Since her father had been a strato-pilot there was probably nothing surprising about this.

Now and again, as she circled in readiness for further attack, she wondered how matters were proceeding in Atlantis. From here the lost city was not visible.

Ethel made up her mind that when she had disposed of her particular 'bag' of monsters, she would head for the lost city and if possible join her Aunt Vi.

She sighted and fired monotonously; then she caught sight of a towering allosaurus scampering alone across the plain 500 feet below. Immediately she began to give chase or at least intended doing so. Instead she found that the machine was dragging to a halt.

Baffled, she stared at the gauges, glanced back at the humming power plant, and then looked outside. An incredible sight forced itself upon her. The remaining five planes of this squadron were stringing upward into the air, some of them tail first as if drawn by an invisible chain. Then the same uncanny attraction seized her own plane.

She snapped on the radio. "Hey, there," she shouted. "What's gone wrong?"

"Magnetism of some sort," came the voice of the commander. "Can't break free. Hang on. Make sure your cabin is sealed in case we're dragged out into space."

Ethel switched off and blundered to the cabin door, satisfying herself it was completely locked. Then, pitched about by the machine's crazy movements, the controls no longer of any use, she stood gripping the window frame and staring outside. The plateau below was already becoming remote. Far away she could see the white square that denoted Atlantis. Then, this too became hidden in cloud.

Higher, faster, up into the stratosphere, and beyond, the six captured fliers sailed into free space. Ethel looked about her on the awesome depths and then shifted her gaze to a distant, gleaming circle like a new penny. There was no doubt that the fliers were being drawn directly toward it for some reason.

Here, in the sealed cabin, she was safe as far as air supply went, and being accustomed to space, it had no terrors for her. What did worry her was the reason for this mysterious 'snatch' and its possible outcome. She could only think that Abna was at the back of it, and this set her wondering if her Aunt Vi had also been captured.

The trip ended with each flier being anchored by magnetism to the space station's spherical side; then orders came over the radio to don spacesuits, leave the planes and enter the space-globe—now repaired after the Amazon's activities—by means of the outer catwalk ladder. The voice was not Abna's. It was colder, harsher.

She scrambled into a spacesuit and obeyed orders. With five other spacesuited forms she mounted the ladder and waited at the interlock between outer and inner walls; then with her colleagues she stepped into the large control room.

Except for the two men at the control switches, there was only one other person present—a tall, thin-faced man of uncertain age with small, intense eyes and a great deal of decoration on his cloth-of-gold suit. He made a motion for the six to open their helmets, which they did; then he said:

"I must apologize for this rather—er—melodramatic method of bringing you here, but it seemed to me the only way. I have the impression that you would hardly have come otherwise. I am Sefner Quorne, adviser-elect to his highness Abna."

"Where is he?" Ethel demanded. "Let us speak to him. He knows me well and he won't tolerate any funny business from you or anybody else."

"He knows you well?" Sefner Quorne considered Ethel pensively. "I do believe you must be Ethel Wilson. How very unexpected, and yet how fortunate."

Ethel looked at him belligerently. "Meaning what?"

"Yes, what?" Barry Schofield repeated, glaring.

"It may help that I have unintentionally captured you, Miss Wilson," the adviser said. "I had not the least idea that you were in the group of fliers which I decided to bring here—"

"Why don't you come to the point?" Barry interrupted. "Where's Abna? We've the right to see him. And I'll tell you something else! You lay a hand on Miss Wilson or say anything out of place to her, and I'll flatten you!"

Sefner Quorne smiled slowly. "How very primitive! And revealing. Plainly you and Miss Wilson must have a very strong bond of relationship for you to behave in this way, for as I observe, you are not nearly so gallant concerning the other ladies in the party."

"Certainly we're friends," Barry retorted. "In fact, we are planning to become engaged shortly."

"Really? My congratulations.... However," Quorne continued, "I am sure that you will be more comfortable without those spacesuits. Let me have them. I assure you that you will not be needing them just yet awhile."

"Look here—" the squadron commander began, but Quorne cut him short.

"Your suits, please! And your weapons!" To obey

was the only course. Quorne's pressure on a button on the wall brought a man into view. He took the space-suits and guns and silently departed.

"That's better," Quorne decided, "and I consider myself most fortunate in that I have at my first attempt succeeded in obtaining three men and three women."

"Tell us what you're getting at," the commander insisted.

"I will. Please be seated." Quorne stepped back and motioned to the chairs screwed into the floor at various points in the control room. When the six had seated themselves, he paced up and down. Then he came to a halt.

"Abna is not here," he said. "At the present moment he will be in Atlantis, I fancy. He discovered that the Golden Amazon had gone there, and so he followed her, which was the chance I have been waiting for. His highness is not aware how much I hate him," Sefner Quorne explained. "Not from any personal standpoint, but because of his authority. Back on my home world he has absolute sway over our male race now that his father is dead. Unfortunately, he is not so ardent a scientist as I. He is young, even romantic, and that can be a big drawback when there is the destiny of a race to consider.

"His Highness has selected the Golden Amazon as the woman he wishes to make his queen. I admire his choice, but for some reason that escapes me, he refuses to use the compulsion he could certainly bring to bear to make her obey him. He tells her of his plans for destroying civilization if she does not wed him, whereas I know he does not intend to put one of those plans into operation. Rather than hurt any of the race to whom the Amazon belongs he would prefer to be beaten. That, however, is not my way.

"His Highness, in my view, has forfeited all right to rule. Once before, when Abna was chasing the Amazon, I had the chance to dispose of his father. With him so obstinate and Miss Brant so uncooperative, I am left with only one alternative. I must destroy them both and take control myself. Back on my home planet I have a powerful clique which can very soon establish mastery of both Jupiter and Earth."

"You can't do anything with the Amazon," Barry said curtly. "She's far too clever for you—and probably Abna is, too."

Quorne smiled. "You think so? When two people are so confused in their emotions as are the Amazon and Abna, their judgment is clouded. I can very soon deal with them. So I propose doing what Abna should have done at first—taking several Earth men and women back to Jupiter and marrying them, their children to form the basis of a new race. So you may consider yourself honoured as being the first in many who will restore life to a race which, through the presence of a deadly disease, has been deprived of its female community."

The squadron commander said: "Supposing you ever got away with this preposterous scheme, what good would it do you? The women would still die, wouldn't they?"

"No. We know now what caused the trouble and have an antidote. We isolated the bacillus that killed all our women, but by then it was too late. The future race will thrive normally."

"I think the scheme's horrible!" Ethel declared angrily, jumping to her feet. "What right have you to dictate to us what we shall do? I demand a—"

"I am afraid, young lady, that you are not in a position to demand anything," Sefner Quorne said.

A man came in swiftly. He murmured a few statements as Quorne listened and then went out again. The adviser considered for a few moments.

"Unfortunately," he commented finally, "I have just been informed that the fliers have now finished the destruction of the prehistoric monsters and have been withdrawn, which will make it extremely difficult for me to obtain any more men or women. To seize them individually is almost impossible unless they are in single planes, as you were. No matter; probably you six will suffice. I think it would be as well perhaps to deal with his Highness and the Amazon and then depart to our home world, leaving behind us a little souvenir to demoralize Earth peoples until the time when we return and take control."

"Just what are you getting at?" Barry asked grimly.

"There are condensor mirrors on this globe which can concentrate sunlight in a burning ray upon Earth. I intend to use them to destroy Atlantis where, at the moment, the Amazon and Abna are—according to telescopic observation upon which I am constantly receiving reports. After that, this space globe will be deserted and we will return to my home—but the mirrors will be left in focus. The result is surely appreciable to you? As Earth turns on its axis the burning track will move across the surface, creating constant destruction wherever it touches—until somebody has the courage to come and see if they can stop it. I know of only one person with such courage—the Amazon. And she will be dead."

CHAPTER SIX
JOURNEY TO JUPITER

With that Quorne motioned and turned aside to the window in front of the control board. The six followed him, not so much because he had commanded it, but because they were sombrely interested in watching his next moves. He gave them a glance and then spoke to one of the two men at the control panel.

"Full focus," he instructed. "Concentrate it on Intersection 19. Which," he added, for the benefit of those looking on, "means this point here."

He indicated a big wall map on which the Earth's western hemisphere was visible. It was crisscrossed by mathematically exact lines, Intersection 19 being exactly across the spot in the Atlantic—as it had formerly been—where the resurrected city of Atlantis now stood.

Quorne turned to a communicator and asked: "Is the Amazon still in Atlantis?" Then when he received the answer, he smiled thinly to himself. Finally he put down the instrument and turned again.

"Evidently she is," he commented. "Her *Ultra* is still outside the city and she has not been seen to leave.

Since his Highness went to join her by instantaneous transportation, it requires no genius to realize that he will be with her. Splendid! Just the way I wanted it."

Ethel half started to say something in bitter protest but Barry cut her short, gripping her arm.

"Save your breath, Ethel," he muttered. "There's nothing you can do."

Quorne asked the men at the controls: "Are you ready?"

"Yes, excellency, everything's prepared."

"Then proceed."

There was a crackling of sparks. Watching through the window, the six saw a concentrated blaze of light, sixteen beams converging into one as they stabbed down toward Earth. The remote speck in the Atlantic where lay Atlantis became hazed in the brilliance and lost to sight.

* * * * * *

The Amazon relaxed against the machine beside which she was standing and gave a cynical smile.

"So you raised Atlantis just to attract my attention?" she asked. "I congratulate you upon your gift for being spectacular, Abna!"

"I tell you it's the truth!" he insisted. "I know you find it hard to believe me, but there it is. If you'll only do as I ask I'll...."

"I have no intention of doing so, and I don't believe your story either!" the girl retorted. She gestured about her. "Great heavens, Abna, you have untold scientific power here—enough to conquer Earth if you set your mind to it. I'd try and stop you, of course, but I doubt if I could manage it. You don't suppose I believe that you're going to throw all this stuff away, do you?"

"Not throw it away. Turn it to peaceful uses. If only I could think of some method by which to convince you!"

"Since it's none of it true, that's impossible. I suppose I am expected to think that now—because I still continue to refuse you—you will fly back to your space station, and perhaps even as far as your home planet, without doing another thing to exert your power?"

"That is precisely what I shall do. But I am hoping that you will change your mind."

"On the contrary, Abna, I intend to return to London, there to gather all my scientific forces to meet you when you try and impose your will by force—and don't try and stop me going either," she warned, levelling her gun. "I'm sorry it has to be this way, but in the absence of proof of your statements it's got to be. You see, you once deceived me and I shall always feel that you can do it again."

Abna clenched his fists but remained silent.

She began backing away. Once she had gained the doorway she started running across the broad terrace in the direction of the street; then she brought up sharp and stared fixedly. For the moment she forgot Abna, her own intentions and everything else in fascination at the sight before her.

Situated as she was at the extreme end of the city she was able to watch its farther reaches crumbling under the heat of a mighty beam of amber light blazing down from the cloudless sky. The white buildings did not explode under it: they fused and crumbled soundlessly, melted by the super heat of sixteen concentrated sunlight beams.

Sudden running footsteps made the Amazon swing around. She gave a grim look as Abna came hurrying toward her. He stopped and stared incredulously at the devouring beam.

"Very clever of you, Abna," the Amazon commented bitterly. "You leave orders behind for your destructive beam to be released, presumably to convince me that you mean what you say. I take it this is your answer to my final refusal to marry you? What did you do? Radio back to your space-globe to release this infernal thing?"

"What time have I had for that?" he asked impatiently. "You have seen all I've done and I came straight away after you." He stood watching the slow destruction of the distant buildings and his eyes narrowed. "This is none of my doing, Vi. It's the work of Sefner Quorne."

"Oh? That adviser of yours to whom I took such a dislike? And where does he fit into it?"

Abna watched the blazing ray as he spoke. "I've had suspicions for some time that he was directly responsible for the death of my father, and if so, it would pay him to get rid of me, too—only I never gave him the chance until I came to Atlantis in search of you. Obviously, he knows I'm here—and probably knows you are, too—so he's trying to destroy the pair of us. Great heavens, Vi!" he broke off fiercely. "You don't think I'd be such an idiot as to destroy my own city like this, do you?"

"Well, no," the Amazon admitted. "Maybe I have been wrong about you after all, Abna, but I'm not saying that because I trust you, but because I heartily distrust Quorne. Anyway, if the idea is to destroy us, he's a good way off the target. We'd better get moving."

"We're safe enough. That beam won't come this way. It's stationary and only appears to move because the Earth is turning— But we have got to get to that space-globe and deal with Quorne before the beam strikes a civilized region, which it will in a few hours."

"Which means the *Ultra*?" the Amazon asked. "You've no way of getting back from that 'instantaneous transportation' trip you made, have you?"

"None."

She motioned Abna to accompany her and they hurried to the *Ultra*.

"It puzzles me," she said, as she settled in the control seat, "why Quorne, if he is trying to destroy Atlantis and us with it, doesn't see that he hasn't done the job properly and move the beam to include all the city."

"It's practically impossible to see from the globe what has happened," Abna responded. "That beam emits a tremendous reflective light which makes the target invisible from the sending end."

As the machine swept up to the stratosphere the girl looked about her upon the empty heavens.

"Apparently those fighter squadrons have gone home," she commented. "Presumably all the monsters have all been dealt with. Queer, though. I expected there would be some of that last squadron we heard at work when we were in that hall."

After thinking for a moment she switched on the radio and was soon talking to Chris Wilson. He listened to all she had to say of her intended visit with Abna to the space station to deal with Quorne; then he broke in:

"You haven't seen Ethel, have you? She and young Barry Schofield are in squadron nine. I haven't heard from them for over an hour and up to then they were sending radio reports pretty regularly. The queer thing is that all the other squadrons have returned reporting that the monsters have all been eliminated."

"I was wondering myself about squadron nine," the Amazon answered. "I don't understand it, Chris. Anyway, I have no time to deal with it now. We'll see what's happened by the time I return from the space-globe, and if Ethel hasn't arrived I'll get busy with an aura-detector."

Abna said: "You'd better take care how you advance when you near the globe, Vi. He's liable to try to blow you out of the universe, chiefly because he'll be pretty certain I'm with you."

"You've got the protonic gun at your elbow there," the Amazon told him. "Better stand by to use it."

He glanced at it and nodded, watching keenly

through the main window as the journey continued. But as the huge globe with its bristling rays came ever nearer—the *Ultra* well to one side of it—there was no sign of hostility. The Amazon began to frown a little.

"Remarkably peaceful," she commented. "Unless he's up to some kind of trickery, or you are," she added suspiciously. "I'm still not too sure of you, Abna."

"Then it's time you were!" he retorted. "I'm not going to argue with you any more, Vi. I've confessed to everything, and if you won't believe me, that's the end of it. You'll see what I mean when we meet Quorne. He can't help but be my open enemy from here on."

"I noticed you managed to repair the breach I made in the wall of the sphere, Abna."

"It was done the moment we got the station back on even keel after you had rammed it. We had to do it: the magnetic force won't work in the plates without them being continuous— Say, Look!" he broke off in amazement.

Almost immediately the Amazon saw what he meant. They had come close enough to the globe by now to observe six single-seated fliers adhering firmly to the outer plates of the sphere, each plane clearly marked with a 'nine'.

"So that's where squadron nine went to," the Amazon exclaimed. "It would seem that your precious adviser snatched them from Earth, Abna."

"Looks like it," he muttered.

The Amazon continued to hurtle the *Ultra* forward, until at last it fell into the attraction of the globe and was drawn with irresistible force to the outer plates where it anchored itself.

"I can soon cut the magnetism off," Abna said, taking spacesuits from the locker. "Come on. We'd better see what's happened."

In five minutes they had crossed from the *Ultra* to the globe. In the central control room there was nobody in sight.

Abna called once or twice, received no response, and then hurried to the control board. He snapped back two switches and the burning ray ceased to operate. Then he left the chamber and was gone for nearly fifteen minutes. When he returned his face was grim.

"Every one of them seem to have cleared out," he announced. "They have left the burning ray in action. Since this globe is poised in an orbit of its own between lunar and Earthly gravity, it follows a course by itself, constantly blasting Earth with the ray, the position changing as Earth revolves and tilts during her seasons. A nice plan!"

"Very," the Amazon conceded sourly. "In other words, Sefner Quorne has taken with him six Earth people, among them Ethel and Barry Schofield, to your own planet, leaving this infernal machine to blast Earth—presumably to terrorize the populace until such time as he can cash in on his terror tactics."

"That's how it looks."

"What do you imagine he'll do now?"

"What I would have done had I been as ruthless as he. He will destroy what remains of my late father's retinue—now my own—and establish himself as the ruler of Vax—or rather Jupiter. As for Ethel and Barry Schofield and the others, the answer is pretty plain. Three men and three women in a race where all the females have died."

The Amazon said: "Our only course now is to pursue Quorne to Jupiter. Were it not for Ethel, I wouldn't make the effort."

Abna said: "I've never been able to understand your tremendous affection for Ethel. After all, she isn't your daughter."

"I know, but she is the kind of girl I would wish for if she were—" The Amazon stopped abruptly, conscious of the fact that she had perhaps spoken her innermost longing too plainly. She saw something of the old mischievous look come to Abna's handsome face.

"Never know," he said drily. "If you married me, you might even have a daughter like her—but far more beautiful, taking after you; and infinitely stronger, taking after both of us."

To kill the conversation the Amazon snapped her helmet back into place so that she could neither hear nor speak, then she turned and marched out of the control room and through the airlock. In a moment Abna followed her, and they only spoke to each other again when they took off their suits in the *Ultra*'s control room.

The machine, with no magnetism holding it to the globe, was already gathering speed for its tremendous journey through the gulf to Jupiter. Behind was the globe with the six abandoned airplanes whirling round its slight mass like baby satellites.

"We have a nice trip before us," Abna said, as he prepared a meal on the small central table. "Jupiter's average distance is four hundred million miles from here. I know because I've covered it—and it's very wearisome."

"Four hundred or four thousand, what's the difference?" the girl asked, shrugging. "I've enough power in the plant to go to the ends of the universe if need be."

They returned to the *Ultra* and after she set the automatic pilot, they sat down to a meal of concentrates.

"How did you make the trip?" she asked. "In the space-globe?"

He nodded. "It also has a small fleet of space-fliers inside it for emergency use. Since one of them has gone, I suppose Quorne took it. Come to think of it, he's only got a few hours start on us, probably. It might even be possible to see him. I'll have a look after the meal."

They both ate in silence for a time, the Amazon aloof and following her own thoughts, so much so indeed that It gave Abna reason to chuckle.

"You surely don't think I'm still trying to pull something, Vi?" he asked amusedly.

"Frankly, no, but I still do refuse to consider our relationship anything more than that of friends. And don't ever forget it!"

His smile faded. "In my own defence, Vi, I would

point out that I am still a gentleman! In case you have forgotten it I am, by descent, the highest dignitary in the Atlantean race. I could have taken advantage of you hundreds of times whilst we have been alone together. I never have, and I never shall—and I'd thank you to remember it!"

The Amazon gazed in surprise and then dropped her eyes to her meal. For just a moment she had glimpsed the real Abna, his pride very much wounded. She had seen the kingly dignity that lay beneath his carefree manner. For perhaps the first time in her life, she felt she had taken—and deserved—an oral thrashing.

Abna said: "You've never been near Jupiter, have you Vi? That is, no nearer than say one hundred million miles. I know you spent some time in the asteroid belt when the sun was dying, which was where I first saw you through our instruments, but of Jupiter itself you know very little, I imagine?"

The Amazon shrugged. "Several unmanned probes were sent out to that region—and way beyond—in the early days of space travel. They sent back a good deal of scientific and astronomical data—but revealed no sign of life. Consequently I've never been as far as the outer planets myself," the girl admitted, "though I hope one day to include them in a federation of the solar system. All I really know about Jupiter is what you've told me—that you and your race occupy the only solid part on his surface, beneath the Great Red Spot, which your ancestors created out of an otherwise hellish world."

Abna nodded. "Outside of our settlement is the most terrifying world you can imagine. Under the Spot we have a gravity which is Earth-normal because of degravitating processes—the same process which raised Atlantis—but out of the influence of our domed city, the real drag of that gigantic planet is felt."

He fell to musing, then continued: "Our city has remained invisible to your probes by polarized light. Outside of its dome, Jupiter has an atmosphere of pure ammoniated hydrogen at frigid temperatures dipping below zero centigrade. Add to that the ceaseless tempests which rage, a gravitation nearly three times stronger than Earth's, vegetation of ammonium carbonate, intensely blue oceans of pure ammonia, and the utterly alien beings who live happily in these conditions of almost eternal night—so far is Jupiter from the Sun—and then you have some idea of the kind of world it is. A horror world, for such as you and I."

The Amazon raised her eyebrows at Abna's casual reference to 'alien beings,' but she did not pursue the topic. Instead she remarked:

"All of which makes me wonder why your ancestors chose Jupiter as a planet on which to settle."

"They chose it because his distance from Earth made him very difficult to study. Thanks to our polarizing dome, no cities can be seen. We did not wish to be disturbed in our new abode."

"You spoke of almost eternal night," the Amazon said. "Hardly that, surely? You have Europa, Ganymede, Io, Callisto, and other large moons; one or other of them always shedding light."

"True, but it struggles to penetrate the immensely deep atmosphere.... I'm telling you all these things, Vi, so you'll know what to expect."

"For that I'm grateful, but why should we bother about them when our destination is your city, hardly different from conditions on Earth itself?"

"I'm thinking of Quorne," Abna explained. "If, in trying to overcome him, we should find ourselves marooned on any part of Jupiter beyond the protective dome, we'll be finished. Both of us are strong, but not strong enough to inhale ammoniated hydrogen and live. Whatever you have endured on other worlds will be as nothing compared to what might happen on Jupiter. The inner planets have conditions pretty similar—but in Jupiter we have the first really alien planet. Of Uranus, Saturn, and Neptune, and far-flung Pluto—I know little, apart from the poisonous compositions of their upper atmospheres revealed by instruments. They're mystery worlds, and if they're anything like Jupiter, they can stay that way as far as I'm concerned."

The Amazon made no comment. Jupiter as yet was no larger than a good-sized pea, his multiple moons strung out in an apparently straight line to either side of him, bright flickerless points.

The Amazon said: "We'd better take it in turns to rest."

"You take the first spell off-duty," he said. "I'll call you in about three hours."

The girl nodded and left him at the control board. In a few minutes she had gained a little chamber she used as a bedroom, and threw herself full length on the bunk. She did not trouble to undress or for that matter to try and sleep. She wanted to think.

What was she to do about Abna? Must she become a woman and admit that she loved him, or remain the cold, calculating scientist and finish her almost eternal life alone in ever-increasing conquest?

Would marrying him make much difference after all? Pooled knowledge, perhaps a child or children in whom she could take an interest, as she had in Ethel.

She found her senses drifting. She was more tired than she had imagined. She watched the First Galaxy swirling into the mist of countless millions of stars and began to breathe deeply. Presently Abna came to the doorway of the little room and looked at her in the starlight.

Coming forward he stooped, kissing her gently and smiled.

"Sorry to take advantage of you, Vi," he whispered, as she remained undisturbed. "But you'd never let me kiss you when you're awake."

The *Ultra* flew on the longest journey it had so far made. The orbit of Mars was passed, and there loomed ahead the empty reaches, dusted with swirling multi-millions of asteroids, remains of a long-exploded planet.

Once through this danger belt, a task which the Amazon handled for herself, flying the *Ultra* above the plane of the veritable 'minefield' of shifting rocks and massive planetoids all balanced against each other and obeying primary laws, there was nothing to impede the path to Jupiter. He had grown now from a pea-sized circle to tennis ball dimensions.

With the flying hours he became like a football, his massive layers of cloud belts plainly visible, and his circular appearance assuming instead the effect of a bulging equator and flattened poles, the inevitable outline of a world still semi-plasmic and bowed out in the centre through fairly rapid revolution.

Fascinated by this view of the giant world, which view she had never seen this close before, the Amazon remained by the outlook ports whenever she could, Abna at her side. Only occasionally did those dense whirling clouds, lashed by the eternal hurricanes forever raging across the planet, part sufficiently to permit of a view of the surface beneath. Then it was one of fantastic rock formations, mainly bluish, or at times a glimpse of the oval Red spot towards which they were steadily heading.

"When we reach the atmosphere, Vi, you'd better let me take over," Abna said.

"Why? There isn't anything I can't do with this machine."

Abna smiled. "True—but I'm accustomed to the gravity, and the winds and I want to be sure that we can land beneath the Spot if at all possible. Remember, there's three times as much gravity and a perpetual wind of something like 400 miles an hour."

The Amazon nodded and accordingly, when the time came, she relinquished her position at the controls.

The instant the *Ultra* plunged into that dense, savagely agitated atmosphere of ammoniated hydrogen, the machine shivered and twisted under the impact, and for a while was borne along helplessly in the grip of the raging hurricane.

It was hard to realize in the insulated quiet of the control room that rank poison swam outside, driven before an everlasting tornado which could have made an Earth hurricane seem like the gentlest of summer breezes by comparison. Nor, as yet, was the tremendous gravitational drag in evidence, since the *Ultra* had its own gravity plates in the floor.

"As near as I can estimate it," Abna said, "the area we want is beyond the mountain range in the distance. Incidentally, there are no mountains on this world higher than 1,000 feet. The gravity stops anything becoming lofty."

CHAPTER SEVEN
THE JOVIAN

The Amazon passed no comment. She was gazing down in wonder on a crystalline jungle, made up entirely of angles, balls, cubes and oblongs after the fashion of frost on a windowpane. It was beautiful and yet ridiculous, a tremendously brittle life of solid ammonia. Even more extraordinary, life was moving amidst this fantastic vegetation, animal in form, thriving in the deadly poison atmosphere.

"Equivalent to Earth animal life," Abna explained, as the girl drew his attention to it. "There's a higher form, too, walking upright like a man: squat, powerful and surprisingly intelligent. The kind of creature who would consider a plate full of smelling salts a first-class dinner!"

The roar of the power plant showed how much current it demanded to raise the *Ultra* in the massive gravity to clear the top of the 1,000-foot barrier. It was accomplished safely, however.

"At the moment you see Jove in his best light," Abna remarked drily. "The sun, distant though it is, does give some illumination, but at night the effect is appalling with only the moons. Since Jupiter turns on his axis every ten hours, there isn't much day or night— Ah!" he broke off. "There's where we want!"

The girl looked ahead to where the greyness of the plain ended in redness. The *Ultra* reached it within a few minutes, and the effect was of gazing down on red sandstone extending for a tremendous distance.

"This is the grey rock solidified by scientific processes," Abna explained. "It can never erupt or otherwise make itself dangerous. It is several thousand miles in diameter, our city and immediate territory taking up eight hundred miles of it under the dome. And there it is!" he finished triumphantly. "A long journey nearly over, Vi."

It looked very similar to the dome that had originally covered Atlantis and, doubtless, was based on the same principle.

"How do you propose getting inside it?" the Amazon asked.

"At the extreme apex there is a movable piece which acts as an airlock. A machine or person can enter it, and an interior lock seals off the air until the pressure is restored, rather like the airlock on a spaceship. The problem is whether Quorne will permit us to enter. I rather think he will, because he knows that if he doesn't we can easily fly away in the *Ultra* and, so to speak, live to fight again another day."

Suddenly the smooth apex of the dome was marred by a huge, oblong, slit inside which was an area of darkness. Gently, Abna lowered the *Ultra* into the hole, waiting for a while as the outer valve closed. Then the lower one moved and he drifted the *Ultra* gently down toward the brilliantly lighted city, presently coming to rest on a wide expanse of soft, earthly looking grass whereon stood half a dozen small-sized space machines and a variety of normal air-fliers.

Suddenly the ever-open radio came to life.

"Welcome, Miss Brant! I assume I am correct in believing I am addressing you? This is Sefner Quorne speaking."

"You're not just speaking to Miss Brant, Quorne, but me as well!" Abna snapped into the microphone. "I've one or two things to say to you! Be in my stateroom in the palace within an hour."

"Certainly, highness."

The Amazon found the palace contained every conceivable comfort and followed the general lines of a high-class hotel on Earth. Abna assigned a suite to her and a couple of servants, whom she promptly dismissed since they were men. She bathed and changed into the Atlantean robes, which Abna had insisted she would find more comfortable during her stay in the city.

In consequence, when at last she emerged from her chamber and walked with regal tread down the long corridor to the stateroom, she was attired in a flowing robe of cloth-of-gold, liberally studded with sapphires and rubies. The long cape she also wore was rather like her own, deep purple on the outside, with a brilliant scarlet lining.

With her golden hair flowing loosely about her shoulders, she finally entered the stateroom where, at the far end, Abna sat in a heavily brocaded chair awaiting her. In the interval he, too, had changed into a golden suit, inscribed with the insignia of his rank.

He watched the Amazon's majestic progress towards him, then rose with a smile.

"Good!" he commented, drawing up a chair for her. "In fact, Vi, perfectly delightful."

"Delightful?" she repeated, inquiry in her violet eyes as she seated herself. "What is?"

"Your general appearance. I always knew you could wear the robes of a queen to perfection. You have the poise, the beauty, the air of authority."

The girl glanced down at herself, then her lips tightened.

"You mean that you offered me these particular robes not so much for me to be more comfortable, but so that I could be dressed befitting a queen?"

"Of course. I felt it might put you in the mood to be more amenable towards me."

The Amazon got up angrily, about to say a good deal, when the arrival of a servant checked her.

"His Excellency Sefner Quorne, highness," he announced, and the adviser came in. He bowed gravely to both Abna and the Amazon.

"My felicitations, your highnesses," he said gravely.

A glint crept into the Amazon's eyes, "If by that, Excellency, you assume that his highness and I are married, you are very much mistaken!"

"Oh?" Quorne seemed surprised. "Forgive me, Miss

Brant. I—er—assumed from the robes that—"

"If you'd stop assuming and do some explaining instead we might get somewhere, Quorne!" Abna said bluntly. "You've plenty to talk about—your heat-ray attack on Atlantis for one thing, in which you obviously hoped to dispose of both Miss Brant and me—and the kidnapping of those six air pilots for another, Miss Wilson and a Mr. Schofield among them. Why did you do it?"

Quorne smiled. "Did you not say yourself, highness, that you would destroy Earth civilization if Miss Brant did not accept your proposition of marriage? I merely carried out your orders. I felt that perhaps she would be more amenable if she saw how much power you really possessed."

"You know perfectly well that I had no intention of carrying out the threats I made. You tried to kill me and Miss Brant, but fortunately you didn't succeed. Nor did you more than scratch Atlantis since the heat-beam was to one side, but the intention was there! As for the three men and women you kidnapped, I suppose you want them to form into marriageable pairs, their children to be the basis for restarting our race?"

"Precisely so, Highness," Quorne agreed, "I cannot see that there is anything illogical about the scheme. In fact, I have closely questioned the three pairs and they are willing to marry, particularly Miss Wilson and Mr. Schofield."

"That's not very remarkable," the Amazon snapped. "They fell in love with each other at first sight, so why should they refuse to marry? And you say the other pairs are agreeable?"

"I—er—have managed to convince them that it is desirable," Quorne smiled. "All three pairs, however, have one objection in common, they do not like the thought of their possible children falling under the dictates of myself for the purpose of building up the race. Understandable, perhaps, but, of course, one cannot be sentimental when the destiny of a race is at stake."

"Your dictates?" Abna repeated, staring. "Where did you get that notion, Quorne?"

"I think I should make it clear, highness, that you are deposed," Quorne explained. "Your continued weakness in tackling the biological issues at the root of our dying race forced me to take action. I had to wipe out the remains of your governing clique, and I am now in complete authority here. You are still a king, but in name only. The people and the servants will only take orders from me.... Not that I harbour any inimical feeling towards either of you—quite the contrary."

Abna said: "I always suspected that you killed my father for your own ends, and now I'm sure of it. The wonder to me is that you allowed Miss Brant and me to enter the dome."

"I did that, highness—or is the title now superfluous?—to assure myself that if you or Miss Brant should happen to find yourselves outside the dome you will not have the protection of the *Ultra*. I propose to take it away from you. You may both stay here as privileged guests for as long as you wish, with absolute guarantee of safety if—and only if—you marry. In that way you can be of service to the community. I regret having to keep emphasizing the necessity for children in our race, but circumstances compel me to."

"Abna already has my answer in that direction," the Amazon said. "I see no reason to alter my decision."

"Even if you did change your mind, Vi, it wouldn't do us any good," Abna said. "You don't suppose I intend to stay here under Quorne's dictates, do you?"

Quorne said: "You leave me no alternative but to be rid of you. Since you will not live together, perhaps you may prefer to die together."

The adviser smiled as he came forward a few paces and considered them—then before he quite realized what had happened it seemed as though something had exploded in his face, and he went flying backward with devastating force. He caught his heel in one of the heavy rugs and toppled over.

Dazed, he looked about him, fingering his aching jaw. He saw Abna towering over him.

"This may not do me much good," Abna said, "but at least it will relieve my feelings. Get on your feet, you lowdown traitor!"

Quorne obeyed slowly, his eyes darting as two guards, who had evidently been listening to the conversation through the door, came hurrying in, their weapons leveled.

The Amazon sprang. Though her flowing robes hampered her movements somewhat, she had her hands free. Her fingers closed with the grip of steel pliers on the back of each man's neck, whirling the pair of them round.

Dizzy with the suddenness of the attack, they had no time to level their guns before they were snatched from their hands. One of the men whirled round with fist raised. The Amazon ducked and slashed up her right and the man fell, his jaw broken.

The remaining man began to back away, but did not reach the door in time to call for reinforcements. The Amazon was upon him in three strides. She slammed him into the wall violently. He could not help rebounding somewhat and, timing it to a split second, the Amazon brought down her clenched fist on the nape of his neck. He slithered to the floor, unconscious.

She hurried to where Abna had Quorne at the point of his own gun.

She said, "Take us to where you have imprisoned the six you kidnapped."

"You leave me little choice, Miss Brant," Quorne responded. "But I warn you that every guard in the city is under my control. You don't suppose you can survive for long once you leave this room, do you?"

"We'll survive as long as I keep this gun on your spine," Abna told him. "If anybody attacks us, I shall shoot you. If you want to preserve your life, for the time being, anyway, you'd better have the guards behave themselves."

With a malignant glance, Quorne led the way down the corridor outside. Here and there, guards were posted. They hesitated, hands on their weapons, then, at the dissuading look they received from Quorne, they relaxed.

The walk to the prison led down one of the main streets, along which there passed many of the male inhabitants. They glanced curiously, but did nothing more. At the main door of the prison at the top of the six steps were several guards.

Quorne walked up three of the steps, then he whirled with lightning speed and snatched the gun out of Abna's hand and hurled it out of reach. Abna lunged savagely but the adviser ducked, yelling at the same time to the guards.

"Wake up, you idiots! Capture these two! Quickly! And no shooting!"

The six men hurried themselves three apiece at Abna and the girl. Abna lost his footing and fell backward to the bottom of the steps. The Amazon found herself seized in powerful hands that strove to force her wrists behind her and so render her powerless. She twisted savagely and one of the men was flung violently away from her. The other two clung on, dragging her down the steps to the level ground where they could deal with her with less difficulty.

Abna struggled up and delivered a bone-splitting blow at the nearest guard. He staggered but, ox of a man that he was, did not fall. The girl for her part feinted with he left, and instead drove her right with all the power she could exert into the nearest guard's stomach. He gasped, purpling as his breath refused to function, then collapsed in anguish on the bottom step.

The Amazon paused a second to tear off her encumbering cape, then she slammed out fiendishly at the two remaining guards. They were wary of her, however, and working in unison, each seized one of her arms and held on tenaciously, bearing her down to the ground at the base of the steps and finally pinning her. Strong though she was, the massive guards crushing each arm proved too much for her.

She lay glaring and shifting futilely. A glance in Abna's direction showed that he, too, was suffering the same treatment, and guard reinforcements were hurrying into view. In the space of a few minutes both the girl and Abna found themselves hauled to their feet, their wrists pinned behind them with coiled lengths of thin, strong chain.

They were conducted by quiet streets and byways to the field where the planes, and the *Ultra*, were still standing. Here Quorne called a halt.

"For your benefit, Miss Brant, I will explain what is intended," he said. "It is our custom with unwanteds to fly them out of the dome to the exterior, and there leave them. Not unprotected, for we have quite a sense of justice—or at least Abna's father—who instituted the regulations, had. You will be provided with space-suits and given oxygen-jet pistols and provisions. Thus equipped, you will be able to fight most of the living perils you will encounter. You can even get to freedom, if you live long enough."

"Freedom?" the Amazon repeated. "That's impossible!"

"Not at all. On your journey here you must have crossed the Eternal mountains. On the summit of one of them is a penal settlement, for outcasts from our race. Perhaps they number 100. They have their own lawless way of living, but at least they are safe. There is food in abundance, light, warmth, everything as it is here, but on a smaller scale—"

"My father had that settlement built," Abna broke in. "It has an airlock entry, as has this dome. His belief was that even criminals deserve a chance so, once turned loose, they could either die on the journey or reach the settlement: it was up to them. They could never return here."

"That being sufficiently clear," Quorne said, "I do not think there is much more to discuss. I will give your best wishes to Miss Wilson, Miss Brant."

The Amazon said nothing. At a signal from Quorne, the guards forced them into spacesuits. Then their gloved hands were tied again, and they were bundled into one of the larger planes.

A pilot settled at the controls, three guards taking up position to the rear of the cabin. The machine climbed swiftly to the summit of the dome. The airlock was opened for them, and then the machine drifted down gently to the red plateau and stopped.

One of the guards opened the cabin's inner door and motioned to the Amazon and Abna to step into the cavity beyond. They obeyed because they had no other course. Reaching to their wrists, he snapped off the clamps that held the chains, and then slammed the door on them. Then the outer door to the red plateau opened and the floor moved beneath them, activated by electric current. Unable to keep their balance, they were thrown outside to the rocks. By the time they had regained their feet, the flier was sweeping up again to the summit of the dome.

The Amazon lowered her gaze and met Abna's eyes through the face-glass of his helmet. By leaning his helmet into contact with hers, he could make the vibrations of his voice travel to her ears.

"What do you think we ought to do?" she asked. "How do we get inside that dome again?"

"The only course that I can see," Abna said, "is for us to go to the settlement and see what tools and equipment the settlers have which might help us smash this dome."

The girl nodded and began to walk forward. Then it was that she discovered what the journey to the mountain range was going to be. She could hardly place one foot in front of the other, so tremendous was the gravitation.

Abna put an arm about her waist and she put one around his. Together they began to flounder forward, then as they emerged from beyond the protection of the dome's bulk, the full fury of the eternal hurricane of Jove smote them.

They both staggered beneath its onslaught, but did not lose their balance. Mightily though it blew, they could still make slow, laborious progress—the reason being that the wind, held by the vast gravity, only equalled the pressure of an earthly gale at perhaps ninety miles an hour.

Steadily, muscles cracking under the effort, they floundered across the red-stone plateau until in perhaps two hours of gruelling advance, they had reached the outskirts of a crystalline jungle. Once inside it the distant view of the frowning hills, greying now with advancing twilight, was cut off. They were still perhaps twenty to thirty miles away.

The trees of the crystalline jungle sprouted branches of much the same pattern as newly woven cobwebs, rings of interlaced, glittering crystal, the outermost edges of the rings being octagonal in shape. Here there was weird, fantastic beauty, every atom of it composed of ammonium base. Even the 'grass' was composed of fantastic spears of glass-like substance that cracked to powder as the pair advanced.

Ever and again, as they stumbled more deeply into the preposterous wilderness, below-zero forms, living by dividing upon themselves in the fission style of a unicell—scudded into safety, looking rather like spiked glass marbles shot through with veins of superb colour.

The Amazon suddenly stopped and her hand flew to her oxygen-jet pistol. Abna saw her action and also halted. He found himself gazing at an incredible creature. He had the contour of a man standing three feet in height and probably every inch as broad. Short, blocky legs were very powerful. His arms too, were short and corded with muscles. To this was added a great barrel of a chest, a neck like a pillar, and a perfectly round head. He had yellow eyes broad nose and a fanged mouth. He had neither hair nor raiment—his entire body seeming to be covered in crystalline scales

"A true Jovian," Abna explained, his helmet touching the girl's. "We've known of them ever since my ancestors arrived on the planet to set up our colony—but they have never shown any desire to interact with us. We've respected that, and gone our separate ways. Don't shoot him, Vi. These creatures are not dangerous. Rather the opposite, and from what I've heard they're pretty intelligent. All the muscles are nature's provision to help him overcome the gravitation."

The creature came forward, his eyes considering them sharply. It was hard for the two in the spacesuits to realize that this creature was breathing pure ammonium carbonate and existing naked in a temperature that plunged below zero centigrade.

Presently he started jabbering. Though Abna and the Amazon had no detectors on their helmets, they heard clearly enough because the super-dense air of the planet carried sound waves with at least four times their normal strength, which in turn penetrated the thickness of the helmets.

"I've not the vaguest idea what he says," Abna commented, touching helmets again. "Since he seems friendly, I might try signs. These creatures are supposed to have the gift of reason. He might be able to help us somehow."

Abna looked about him and finally selected a clear

stretch of red ground nearby. With the needle-thin jet of his oxygen-pistol he began to draw on the rock. He drew the dome, marked the airlock on the top of it, and then pointed to himself and the girl. Then by further signs he showed that they wished to enter the dome. To his amazement, he heard a reply as though the Jovian had spoken it.

"What you mean is that you and your friend are shut out of the dome and want to get back inside it?"

The Amazon looked at Abna blankly. Abruptly the face of the Jovian split into a grin.

"I read your mind," he explained. "Both your minds. I'm concentrating thoughts at you and they take the form of the language you understand."

"But telepathy is an extremely exact science," the Amazon mused to herself, and her thoughts evidently reached the squat, enormously powerful being for he turned to her.

"To you, perhaps, who have developed other means of communication, such as sound. We, you will notice, have no ears. That is nature's provision to prevent us being deafened by the vibrations in this heavy atmosphere. Since we have not developed sound in our race, we have developed telepathy instead, and can read each others' thoughts quite easily, as I can read yours."

"But you shouted just now," Abna pointed out. "We heard you."

"Certainly I shouted to see if you understood. I could not hear myself, but it occurred to me that you might. I know now it was a waste of time. Thought-transference is so much easier."

"I don't understand this at all," the Amazon said, moving forward to peer at him more closely. "You have a gift like telepathy, and yet spend your time roaming wild in this jungle. Why have you and your race not built cities, mastered science, and made yourselves rulers of the planet?"

Again the Jovian grinned. "Why? Because we are a lazy race. We don't want to progress. We understand most scientific things, but are not interested enough to develop them. Our theory is that the more refined you become, the less happiness you have."

"Is there any way in which you can help us?" Abna asked. "We have got to get back inside the dome somehow—back to our own race."

"Who have unjustly thrown you out," the Jovian added. "I can read your thoughts, remember. Yes, I think I can help you. What do you think those inside the dome would do if they saw a vast pillar of fire blazing steadily into the night?"

"Normally, they wouldn't," Abna responded. "The dome blocks all light-waves. However, the lookout, watching through a non-polarized screen, would probably report the incident and there'd be an investigation. But where does the pillar of fire come from?"

"It is a simple matter of chemistry," the Jovian explained. "You have pistols which fire a destructive jet of pure oxygen. Were you to fire into pure hydrogen— so rarely met with in its isolated state—a tremendous explosion and fire would result."

"We know that," the Amazon said. "Just an ordinary law of physics that hydrogen and oxygen are violently explosive in contact, but in this atmosphere, hydrogen is not the main constituent. Ammonia plays a big part."

The Jovian motioned to the ghostly interlacings of crystalline trees.

"Those," he said, "are filled with hydrogen. Watch this effect. Give me your gun please."

Abna hesitated and the Jovian grinned.

"You don't trust me, eh? You should. I'm the only one who can help you. If you are so much in doubt, my friend, have your lady companion cover me while I demonstrate."

CHAPTER EIGHT
ESCAPE

Abna nodded and the Amazon focussed her pistol just in case. The Jovian took the weapon, reached out with his free hand, and snapped off a brittle crystalline branch. Then he turned the jet pistol upon it. Instantly the jungle clearing was lighted with blinding brilliance as sizzling explosive fire consumed the branch—not in one explosion but with a sputtering, crumbling intensity as the ammonia in the atmosphere, slow to combine, acted as a damper.

"You see?" the Jovian asked, handing the pistol back. "With a small heap of these branches you can create a pillar of glaring fire which will certainly bring some-body from the dome to investigate. They will have to use a plane because of the dome's height. Once they are within your reach your problem is solved. You have only to act."

The Amazon and Abna began breaking off branches and then starting their wearying, crushing struggle to transport the stuff to within a mile of the dome. The Jovian was quick to see their difficulty and before they could realize what had happened, he became a tornado of energy, covering the journey back and forth at least a dozen times in the period it took them to travel the single distance.

They arrived breathless and with aching muscles, to find a pile of broken crystalline branches nearly six feet in height in a rough pyramid. The Jovian surveyed it in the fitful light of the moons and grinned.

"That should do it, my friends," came his thoughts. "I warn you to look in the opposite direction when you ignite the stuff. It will be unbearably brilliant."

"Before we do light it," the Amazon said, "our thanks are due to you for the way you've helped us. I certainly didn't expect to encounter on Jupiter anybody so friendly and cooperative as you have been."

"No virtue in it." the Jovian responded. "With nothing to gain by helping you I might just as well assist. But I must leave you here. I have my wife, as you would call her, and children to join. They are expecting me back with food."

He grinned widely and strode off into the shadows.

Abna pressed the button of the pistol and at the same moment looked away. It was as well he did so for the crystalline branches instantly ignited and hurled a pillar of fire twenty, fifty, one hundred feet into the night, illuminating the mile-distant dome with intense brightness and drenching the red plain in magnesium clear brilliance for a tremendous area. Motionless, Abna and the girl lay on their faces, turned away from the glare, watching the dome.

Being latently combustible, the fire maintained its

intensity steadily as the seconds passed, seconds which seemed like hours to the watching pair. Then they saw a plane sweeping down from the apex of the dome, alighted no more than a dozen yards away, but nobody emerged.

"They're studying it," Abna said, his helmet again touching the Amazon's. "It's possible they won't emerge because it means the bother of spacesuits. They can see what the fire is and that may satisfy them. Come on, we've got to get that plane."

He struggled up, gun in hand, and aided the girl to rise. With cumbersome movement, guns levelled, they moved towards the flier. It occurred to both of them as they advanced that they must be in full view, but no weapons were aimed at them. Presumably the pilot was so absorbed by the crystalline fire that he had failed to notice the pair approaching from one side.

The moment he gained the plane Abna pointed his gun through the glass side of the cabin, tapping on the dense glass. The brilliantly lighted face of the pilot turned and looked at him, startled.

Instantly he grasped the situation and dived his hands at the switches. Abna struck the glass with his gun, using all his massive strength. It powdered it. Two more savage blows made a hole in it. He had no need to fire. The pilot within died instantly as the air was replaced by the ammoniated hydrogen from outside.

Abna gave the Amazon a grim glance in the light of the now waning fire, then together they smashed away the remainder of the window and clambered through the frame into the cabin. The body of the dead pilot they tossed outside to the plateau Abna touched his helmet to the girl's.

"I'd no intention of killing him, but it was him or us, and this time it's got to be us. We'll get inside the dome now, I think, since they'll assume it's the pilot coming back—but what will happen after that I don't know."

He threw the switches, and the machine rose to the height of the dome and dropped into the cavity below the open outer airlock. There was the usual pause while the pressure was regulated, then the lower lock was opened and Abna guided the machine slowly across the city. As he did so, he pushed back his helmet on its hinge and motioned the girl to do likewise. It gave them the opportunity to speak normally.

"Any suggestions?" he questioned. "Once I bring this plane down again at the airport we'll be captured once more."

"Cruise for a moment while we think it out," the girl said quickly. "Those in charge will wonder why you're doing it, of course, but we've got to have time to make a plan."

Abna shifted the controls slightly and the machine began to bank off to the left, sweeping so high over the city that it nearly touched the inner side of the dome. The Amazon stood by the window, looking intently in the direction of the distant airport.

"The *Ultra*'s still where I left it," she said. "We could easily fly to it and escape, if we could penetrate this dome with our initial takeoff."

"Quite easily. From the inside this dome is breakable but not from the outside. If you smashed it, though, you'd kill everybody in the city. The ammoniated atmosphere would sweep in."

"So it would!" The girl swung, her violet eyes gleaming. "Abna, is that worth thinking about? If we can do it, we can wipe out Quorne and indeed everybody."

"Including Ethel and the others," Abna pointed out. "You surely don't want that?"

"Naturally not. We must rescue them; then we're ready to make a getaway, if we can. Is there anybody in this race whom you would wish to save? Or are you prepared to let them all be destroyed?"

Abna considered this as he cruised the plane around.

"As usual, Vi, you are completely ruthless," he said. "But in this case I agree with you. All those who stood for justice—those who comprised my late father's retinue—have been wiped out by Quorne. The remainder are loyal to him, or else under his dictates. And what he stands for is conquest at any price. First of all Jove, then Earth, then the planets you have annexed in the name of Earth. Yes, they're all better annihilated. I am prepared to make Earth my abode, where my race originally existed."

"That settles it then," the Amazon said. "Now, how to save Ethel and the others? Presumably they'll still be in the prison?"

"Presumably. If the Atlantean law is being followed, they will not be married for another week, so until then they'll certainly be kept in captivity."

The Amazon looked out over the city. "Which building is the prison?"

Abna indicated the massive isolated building in the city centre. The girl looked at it for a while and then said:

"Our only chance is to get to the *Ultra* and then fly in it to the prison. The *Ultra* has weapons in it that can smash the doors or fuse the walls, giving us the opportunity to enter. The chances are that Ethel will see the *Ultra* and know we're aboard. Once she gives some kind of signal, we can go straight to where she is and get her, with the others."

"She's not the only one who'll know we're aboard the *Ultra*," Abna remarked. "Quorne and his men will be after us like lightning."

"We can deal with them, I think, unless they try something four-dimensional."

"They won't do that. It would be too dangerous within the confined space under this dome. We'll risk it," Abna decided briskly, and set the course of the machine for the airport.

In a matter of minutes the machine landed within yards of the *Ultra*. Two guards were standing near it, evidently keeping a watch until Quorne decided what was to be done with it. Abna scrambled out of the deflated folds of his spacesuit.

"Nothing for it but bare fists, Vi," he said, as she too emerged from her spacesuit to appear still clad in her queenly robes. "These oxygen pistols are no use inside the dome. If you're ready, I am."

The distance of the flier from the *Ultra* was perhaps fifteen yards and at the moment the guards, lax in their duty, were standing talking together, ignoring the plane that had just arrived. They were assuming, of course, that the pilot who had recently departed in it had returned to report. Abna plunged outside and streaked towards the *Ultra*. The Amazon followed him, finding her robes a hindrance, but in no more than a dozen strides she reached the nearest guard while Abna tackled the farther one.

Neither man had a chance to do anything. Struck down with iron fists they collapsed in the dust of the airfield. By the time they had recovered their scattered senses, the *Ultra* was rising with graceful smoothness, the Amazon at the controls, darting it quickly towards the prison. Abna took the powerful proton gun in readiness for defensive action.

In three minutes the prison was reached. The girl circled the *Ultra* about it in a tight circle, watching keenly for a signal from one of the barred windows. It came at last from a topmost window—the movement of something white, perhaps a handkerchief. Instantly the Amazon swung to Abna.

"Blast the top off the parapet over that window," she ordered. "Make room for them to get out without dropping masonry on top of them. I'll keep you centred as near as possible."

He swung the proton-gun round, focussing on the required spot on the building. The stream of energy he hurled forth fissured and then dissolved the stone-work over the window into a gummy, sizzling plasma. He tried again, keeping the gun trained with difficulty as the *Ultra* was compelled to keep shifting position. Little by little he dissolved the wall at the top and around the window until, evidently shoved mightily from inside, the whole mass of bars and framework fell out and down into the street. As the *Ultra* swept by the gap there was a vision of six waving people, no roof over their heads.

"Better hurry," Abna said. "I've just spotted about a dozen fighters rising from the airfield."

The Amazon switched in the rotary blades so that they emerged from the *Ultra*'s roof and permitted the machine to hover, helicopter-style, ever nearer the building. When she had inched reasonably near enough for a leap to be made, she moved the remote control switch for the airlock, and it opened.

In a few seconds the six prisoners, led by Barry Schofield, had leaped the narrow gap and tumbled into the control room—just as the door slammed and the *Ultra* rocked under the impact of vibratory beams from the fliers now swarming around like wasps. Two of them went down before Abna's proton-gun.

"They can't penetrate this armoured hide," the Amazon said. "Hang on, everybody!"

She lowered the helicopter screws, moved over the power lever and threw all the energy she dared into the plant. The machine darted upward with such violence that everybody, including Abna, was flung helplessly to the floor—and there remained, pinned by the tremendous acceleration.

Her jaw set, her back crushing into the springs of the control seat, the Amazon watched the mighty glass dome overhead sweeping to meet her. Instinctively she threw a forearm over her eyes as with the shattering impact the nose of the *Ultra* struck the barrier.

The machine jarred, rocked, swirled crazily—then went on, higher and higher, up into the surging hurricane, into the blankness of the eternal clouds, fighting back now both elements and the appalling Jovian drag.

The speed slowed down gradually though the power was working at full pressure. Infinitely far below, the riven dome swirled out of sight. Mile by mile the Amazon fought the machine upwards, out beyond the cloudbanks at last and into the light of the multiple moons; then very slowly she eased off the frightful pressure and began to breathe a little more freely.

They were clear of Jupiter, and with every hundred miles his colossal power was weakening. Abna got up off the floor and helped the others to rise. Not having his strength, they lay about on the wall couches or in the chairs fighting for consciousness and forced the air into their lungs.

Then they began to notice that the strain was dying away as, the distance from Jupiter constantly increasing, the automatic gravity plates in the floor had a chance to function.

Ethel was the first to speak. She went over to the Amazon as she sat at the control board charting the course.

"I knew I could rely on you, Aunt Vi," she said eagerly. "I kept telling them that in prison. That horrible creature Quorne came and told us that he'd sent you and Abna outside the dome and that you'd never come back."

Abna looked out on the wilderness of space.

"Nobody following," he said. "Not that there would be time, I suppose, before the ammonia gas swept in. In that moment, Vi, you finished what remained of my race."

"Any regrets?" she asked briefly.

"None. I told you that. This seems to be about the end of the business, Vi. Except for those in the penal colony, about whom we don't need to think again, only I am left of Atlantis. All we have to do now is return to Earth. Everything's come to such a sudden stop I can hardly credit it."

The Amazon gave her faintly cynical smile. "And, Abna, in case you don't realize it yet, I've beaten you! Completely! When you agreed that your race should be destroyed, you also admitted there was no purpose in your race continuing, therefore no need of our marrying. No need of children. You cut the ground from under your own feet."

"I suppose I did," he admitted. "I knew what I was doing, though. Quorne had to be destroyed and those with him. But I haven't given up the idea of your marrying me. I'm hoping you will someday. Not with any ideas about perpetuating my race, but because we have so much in common and because I still love you."

The Amazon said nothing. She got up and went to the table, settling down at the meal of concentrates prepared by Ethel. Abna joined her at the opposite end of the table.

Ethel said: "I've often wondered how you'd look, Aunt Vi, in the robes of a queen instead of that black fighting suit or ordinary civilian attire. Now I know. And you look marvellous! Doesn't she, Barry?"

"To my mind the Amazon would look marvellous no matter what she wore," Barry Schofield said.

"As for these robes," the Amazon said, "they were wished on me. I didn't choose them."

"Then you should," Ethel said promptly. "You've no idea how regal they make you look. After all, why not? You are the dictatress of the inner solar system."

"She could be dictatress of the entire solar system if she'd listen to me," Abna said. "Jupiter and his retinue of moons is now in line for colonization. The larger ones, such as Io, could quite easily be given atmospheres and made habitable. My race never did so because the transformation would have been seen from Earth, but now there is no barrier. Then there are Saturn, Uranus, and Neptune waiting to be opened up."

"You said king and queen, Abna," the Amazon reminded him. "That would be very different to dicta-tress."

He shrugged. "You have secrets I have not—and vice-versa. It would be a 50-50 affair—but what's the use?"

After a brief silence the squadron leader spoke.

"What about that space-globe, Miss Brant? Is it still where it was, circling the Earth with a burning ray?"

"The ray was switched off," the Amazon told him. "The globe itself is still there and it might be turned to good use. If we took it farther into space, it could be used as a halfway station between Earth and Mars, as well as one of the finest cosmic observatories ever created. You agree, Abna?"

"A good idea," he assented. "We'll have a look at it as we return home and see what we can do. There is also another point to be considered—my official status. I'm a ruler without a race, which is unprecedented in history. I could overcome the difficulty by marriage to you, Vi, but since you won't have that, I have only one other course—revive what is left of Atlantis from the ray attack and live there."

"You mean you don't intend to become one of the community?" the Amazon asked in surprise.

"Yes, I could do that. Revive the scientific machines—"

"And perhaps become a menace?" the Amazon asked. "No, I won't allow that."

"You may find it difficult to stop me."

"You can't just live there by yourself!" Ethel protested.

The Amazon said: "We'll discuss that aspect when we're nearer home. For the moment I think we might do worse than try and get some sleep, one of us remaining on guard."

* * * * * * *

Several Earth days later the space-globe had again been reached, and the *Ultra* chained to the globe by reason of its superior mass. As the party stood in the main control room of the globe the Amazon nodded decisively.

"Yes, with most of it converted into restrooms, solariums, amusement centres, and so forth, this can be made a useful halfway point. It only requires moving to a spot approximately twenty million miles from Earth, halfway to Mars. You agree, Abna?"

"I might as well since you've annexed the thing."

"The spoils of battle," the Amazon told him. "At least I shall use it in the cause of peace and comfort, which is more than your adviser did—or you either, recalling the havoc of restoring Atlantis. Those mirror-condensers will have to be dismantled, of course, and—"

She stopped talking, looking about her in amazement as the entire globe suddenly began to shift position crazily and they were all thrown from their feet.

Abna fought his way on hands and knees across the floor to the window. With a strain that brought bulging veins to his forehead, he half stood up and stared outside, supporting himself by the elbows on the window ledge.

The Earth below was receding so rapidly that it was obvious the space-globe was falling 'upwards' with tremendous velocity. And with every second the velocity was increasing, sending the enormous globe hurtling in the direction of the Moon's orbit.

The Amazon, breathing hard with exertion, fought her way to Abna's side and gazed with him.

"How do you explain it, Abna? We haven't touched anything in here to cause this globe to move. It was naturally poised by gravitation at 20,000 miles from Earth, wasn't it?"

"That's right. There's only one answer I can think of. Somebody is directing a force beam at us from Atlantis and it's flinging this globe outward into space. There are machines in Atlantis for generating such a beam, in the part of the city which was not destroyed."

"But who could be doing that?"

"It begins to look as though we guessed wrong when we thought we'd finished with Quorne, Vi," Abna said. "I can't think of anybody but him being responsible for this."

"But it's impossible! We've crossed space at a tremendous speed from Jupiter. He couldn't possibly have overtaken us, reached Earth, and resurrected Atlantean equipment in that time. And, besides, he must have died with the rest of your race when the gas surged into the dome."

"For the moment," Abna confessed, "it's a mystery." He turned and staggered heavily toward the switchboard.

"There should be a degravitator switch somewhere here," he said. "It'll cut out the inertia, though it won't stop us moving."

He presently found it and pulled it down hard.

Instantly the vast pressure relaxed, almost too much so. The six on the floor again to float ceilingward and kicked helplessly. Abna slowly adjusted the power pointer until he had the gravity operating normally in ratio to the acceleration.

He said: "What we have to do now is break free of this force beam, and that won't be easy. To the best of my knowledge the beam has a radius of 200 million miles before it starts to lose efficiency. Which means we could be hurled that far before we could break away."

"And which will carry us far beyond the orbit of the Sun and into the outer depths of space," the Amazon said.

CHAPTER NINE
END OF ATLANTIS

She returned to the window and studied the view. Earth was still shrinking rapidly. The orbit of the Moon had been passed and they were hurtling toward Venus, but well to the side of it. Trailing the globe at a constant distance was the *Ultra*, still chained by the mass.

The squadron commander made a suggestion. "Would it do any good if we got out of the globe into the *Ultra* and then drove the *Ultra* away, like a lifeboat from a sinking ship?"

"It might work...," The Amazon started to say, but Abna cut her short.

"It would mean that the force beam would strike us, since it envelops this globe, as we jumped to the *Ultra*. We'd either be disintegrated or hurled through space at such a pace we'd die almost instantly. Out there we wouldn't have gravity-nullifiers as we have in here."

Abna sat down at the table and began to figure rapidly on a scratch pad. After a moment or two he glanced up and smiled a little.

"Here is a problem you cannot solve, Vi," he said, "but I can. We can escape by using the fourth dimension."

The Amazon did not respond. Her lack of knowledge in regard to the fourth dimension had long been a sore point with her. She moved to Abna's side and looked over his shoulder at a mass of symbols and equations. Some of them she understood: most of them she did not.

"This space-globe is equipped with four-dimensional apparatus for defensive purposes," Abna explained. "It is just possible by converting the apparatus, that we might be able to create a four-dimensional shield round this globe. That would have the effect of deflecting the force beam from a straight line. In other words, it would be bent at an angle. Four-dimensionally, light can be forced out of a straight line—so then can other radiations, force being of the same order."

Apparently nobody save the Amazon could grasp what he was driving at. Even she found it difficult to comprehend a science out of her ken. Nevertheless she nodded promptly enough.

"I'll help you with whatever's necessary, Abna."

He rose and crossed to the mathematical computers, which were capable of incorporating a fourth dimension in their output. Ethel, Barry, and the remainder of the party could only look on and wonder at the technical skill of Abna and the Amazon as they started to dismantle the equipment, Abna giving directions as the work progressed.

Two hours passed while this was done, and in that time the hurtling globe had fled across the orbit of Venus and was streaking on to the final orbit of Mercury, after which the Sun alone was left to be reckoned with.

Ethel, taking instrument readings at the Amazon's request, found that they were still some thirty million miles from the orb of day.

"Which gives us time," Abna commented. He carefully studied the work that had been executed and then laid his hand on the master switch. Turning, he added, "When I close this switch, the four-dimensional effect should operate, and apart from deflecting the force beam harmlessly into space, it will also produce uncanny effects with light waves. You will see what I mean by looking on the heavens with the four-dimensional shield intervening."

The party moved to the window to watch, then they gasped a little in amazement as they saw what Abna meant. The glittering points of the stars changed to curiously 'faded-off' rods, rotating oddly about a centrally brilliant fulcrum. The sun lost his brightness and instead assumed the appearance of a scooped-out bronze bowl. Light waves themselves were vaguely visible, but not moving in straight lines. They were curved and even rectangular.

Little by little Abna eased the globe out of position, edging sideways. By a study of the instruments, he knew when he had shifted out of the grip of the force beam. Only then did he close the switch that created the four-dimensional effect, and the heavens snapped back into their normal appearance.

For several moments Abna was silent, then he nodded in satisfaction.

"Done!" he announced triumphantly. "We've slowed our speed right down, and now we're starting to move away from the Sun and back toward the Earth. The force beam has completely lost us."

"Will that fact be evident to whoever is operating it?" the Amazon asked.

"Possibly. Instruments should show that the object against which the beam was pressing is no longer there. It will be left to whoever the operator is to decide how we escaped. He may even think that we have been flung into the Sun and that his job is done, though I hardly think so. However, he can't find us again. We're far beyond normal telescopic range and I don't think detectors are trained on us. In case they are," Abna added, "I'd better take precautions."

He closed another switch on the complicated board. Outside the ports the heavens completely vanished, including the Sun. It was as if the space globe were sealed inside a totally black void. Yet it cast no reflections from the lights shining through the portholes.

"Invisibility?" the Amazon questioned.

"Yes. A light-polarizing shield completely encircles this globe. Similar to the dome we had over the city on Jupiter."

"And when we start nearing Earth, what do you propose doing?" the Amazon continued. "Whoever this person is, he has go to be dealt with."

"I'm afraid there is only one thing for it, Vi," Abna

said. "Though it grieves me quite a lot, I'll have to destroy Atlantis. Bury it under the sea, complete with its machines and if possible drown the person who's back of this attack."

"But you said you were going to live in Atlantis!" Ethel exclaimed.

"I know, but if this person has control of Atlantis he's extremely dangerous. Not only to us, but to everybody on Earth. For all we know, he may even now be releasing engines of destruction against Earth people in the hope of conquering them. There can be no peace until he is stopped, and since it is impossible to get near him while he rules those machines the only course is to obliterate them, and him."

There was a silence for a moment, then Barry Schofield spoke.

"I think you're right, Abna. There's no other way to be certain."

"Which will make it that you will have to become one of the normal community after all," the Amazon pointed out. "You won't like that."

Abna gave her a direct look. "Doesn't it occur to you, Vi, that I am making this sacrifice, destroying Atlantis and all its valuable equipment, just to save your people? I haven't even considered my own position in the matter. What more proof do you want that I'm genuine in my desire to cooperate with you?"

"I appreciate the cooperation," the Amazon responded. "And I don't see why it can't remain that way without marriage."

Abna dropped the subject and turned again to the instruments.

* * * * * * *

When at length the globe returned to its former position at 20,000 miles from Earth and Abna had it once more balanced in its orbit, he cut off the invisibility shield for a while and studied Earth through the telescopic devices, getting his bearings. The instant he had them he returned the invisibility shield into position.

"From the look of things," Abna said, "Atlantis is not operating at the moment and there don't appear to be any signs of chaos on Earth as there would be from destructive attack. Nonetheless I'm going to return Atlantis to the depths, with regrets. It's a simple process; merely a reversal of the degravitating method which raised it."

"There'll be plenty of catastrophe when that return to the depths takes place," the Amazon remarked. "The Oceans will flow back into position; there'll be earthquakes, general upheaval."

"True, but they cannot in any way equal the chaos which was caused when the water was hurled back. In fact, the return of the water to normal levels will be of benefit. The floods throughout the world will subside."

Turning to the control panel, he closed the switches that set the power plant humming strongly. It maintained its steady rhythm for perhaps ten minutes and then silence returned. The invisibility shield was turned off and the party gazed toward the Earth 20,000 miles below.

Turbulence was visible and tormented clouds caused by violent atmospheric changes as great bodies of water shifted position, but gradually through the confusion it became obvious that the strip of territory which had joined America and Europe had disappeared and the ocean was back in its place.

"Which makes me a ruler without a race and without a home," Abna said with a grave smile. "Since in many ways my science is the equal—and superior—of yours, Vi, I think you'll have to take me into your government."

"Willingly," she agreed promptly. "That was what I wanted from the first. Forget Atlantis, forget your race, and use your science alongside mine."

She turned to the switchboard and set the radio in operation.

"Violet Ray Brant calling Earth," she intoned. "Violet Ray Brant calling. Contact Mr. Wilson of the Dodd Space Line. Hello!"

"Message received," came a voice. "You are connected, Miss Brant."

"Hello there, Vi," came Chris Wilson's tones. "I was beginning to wonder what had happened to you. What about Ethel? I haven't had any news of her since—"

"She's here, and safe," the Amazon interrupted. "Quite a few things have been happening. I'll give you the details later. First, I want to know how things are on Earth."

"The most interesting thing at the moment is that

I have just had news that Atlantis has subsided into the ocean, taking the entire Murian continent with it. I don't begin to understand it."

"We're responsible for that," the Amazon replied and sketched in the details. "How much damage was caused?"

"Hardly any. In fact quite the contrary. The floods have gone down with miraculous speed, which is the very thing we needed."

"You haven't been under attack from Atlantis during my absence?"

"No." Chris sounded puzzled. "Why should we have been?"

"I just wondered. Apparently somebody with a mighty good reason tried to be rid of Abna and me—and those with us—but we managed to overcome the trouble—or rather Abna did with four-dimensional tactics. It is possible that that danger has now gone since we've sunk Atlantis back into the ocean. What I want you to do, Chris, is send a dozen guards out to this space-globe immediately to watch over it. They must also bar the spaceways and examine every machine that leaves Earth. There is a chance our unknown attacker may have escaped Atlantis and will try to get away now his weapons have been taken from him. You'll do that?"

"I'll do it right away. What are you planning to do?"

"Return to Earth and try and get things on in even keel again."

The Amazon rose from the control-chair and turned

to face the party.

"Spacesuits, everybody," she instructed. "We have to be ready to take over the *Ultra* when the guards arrive, and so back to Earth."

All save Abna turned to the locker room where the suits had been placed. He seemed to be lost in thought and presently caught the Amazon's eye.

"I'm puzzled," he admitted. "I can't understand why, with all that apparatus in his power, Quorne didn't try to subjugate Earth since he was reasonably sure he had rid himself of you and me in this space-station."

"Perhaps he wasn't so sure," the Amazon pointed out. "He may have known we dodged that force beam. You've no idea of his aura number?"

"His what?"

The Amazon smiled a little. "This is where my science comes into play again instead of yours. I long ago perfected an aura-compass. It has a needle that turns to any particular aura I desire, just as the ordinary compass needle points to the magnetic pole. Every living thing has a different aura."

"I've rarely dabbled in that kind of science."

The girl became silent, obviously thinking hard over the problem. She did not refer to it again until she and the remainder of the party were back once more in the *Ultra*'s control room and heading for Earth, the dozen guards having been left in charge of the space-globe.

"It occurs to me," she said, "that there may be a point in our favour concerning the aura-detector. I know that no Earth aura ever exceeds 5,000. That may be peculiar to Earth people. It is just possible that an earlier race—such as you are, Abna, and such as Quorne is— might have widely different aura frequency. Just let me see what your aura is before I theorize further."

"Willingly," Abna agreed. "What do you want me to do?"

"Just hold this in either hand." The Amazon handed him an instrument like a voltmeter with two electrodes on either side of it. "You will complete the circuit of your radiation, and the needle will register it, stop-watch fashion."

Abna nodded and followed instructions. Then he handed it back, looking at the reading over the girl's shoulder.

"8,002!" she exclaimed. "That's well worth knowing! No normal Earth person has an aura like that. Evidently you of Atlantis have a higher reading than our people. What I shall do upon return to Earth is set to work with a general detector. It will be devised so that when it strikes a person with an aura above 5,000, which cannot possibly be a normal Earth person, it will record the fact and the exact position of the person at that moment. In that way we can find out where Quorne is, if he's alive and automatically work out his aura. In other words, a scientific detective."

An hour later she brought the *Ultra* down safely at the spaceport in central London.

"For the time being this is where we split up," she said. "You, Ethel, had better get along home and put your mother's fears at rest: I'll tell your father where you are. You, Barry, will have to report to your flying unit and so will the rest of you. You, Abna, had better come with me to my headquarters, where I can decide how you fit into the scheme of things."

He accompanied her to the rank of air taxis, and one for the use of government officials rapidly transported them to the executive building where Chris Wilson was profuse with his greetings. Then he realized that the Amazon was wearing regal robes.

"Does this mean—?" he began to ask, but she cut him short.

"It certainly doesn't, Chris, and the sooner I get rid of these encumbrances, the better I'll like it. First, though, I have something I must do. You carry on for the time being, Chris. Ethel's okay. I packed her off to her mother. Abna, come with me."

He followed her into the adjoining laboratory and looked about him upon the instruments. A half-tolerant smile came to his lips.

"That's one thing in you that annoys me, Abna!" the Amazon snapped as she noticed his expression. "Your air of being so patronizing. I know there are some machines here which are child's play to you, but there is one which is obviously not—my aura-detector apparatus."

As she sat down at the big instrument he watched her fingers as she played on a matrix keyboard.

"It baffles me," he confessed. "What sort of results are you getting?"

"Nothing yet. This may be a long job if Quorne has

left the immediate vicinity of the city and gone to some other part of the world."

Abna drew up a stool and settled himself to wait. An hour passed. Then the recording needle swung to 8104 and became steady. Instantly the girl cut off the power and the needle remained fixed in its position.

"Got it!" she exclaimed, her eyes gleaming. "And it looks as though your guess about Quorne was right, Abna. If it's not him, it's certainly an Atlantean. I must calculate exactly where he is."

She pressed a button that set the needle swinging in its vacuum case. After a second or two's movement it came to rest and, each swing giving exact mileages, and the needle's direction the compass bearings, it was not a difficult matter to deduce where the owner of aura 8104 existed.

"There!" the Amazon said, standing up and pointing to a spot on the huge map of London. "To the east if the Thames. That area in these days is mostly devoted to dwellings for the workers who are rebuilding the city. Rather a strange place for such a dignitary as Quorne to live. I must investigate."

"I'll go with you," Abna said, rising.

"No." The girl shook her blonde head. "This is my party, Abna. When anything goes wrong on this planet I deal with it, and nobody else."

She went swiftly to her own quarters in the building, where she quickly changed from her regal robes into her everyday Amazon costume, and a short time later donned blue overalls specially grimed for the purpose.

Her thick golden hair she screwed into a knot and secured it firmly inside a worker's cap.

For the rest, a dark cream changed the hue of her skin from yellow to dirty white. Only the deep violet of her eyes gave her away. She considered them in the big mirror for a while and finally slipped contact lenses into position, designed to give the impression of a grey iris. Thus disguised, nobody could have looked less like the Golden Amazon, particularly in the slouching walk she assumed as she left the room, and the building.

To her wrist she had attached a small aura-compass set to the reading of 8104 and it guided her infallibly. Without using any vehicle she walked to a workers' quarter of the city—an area left bare after the retreat of the great glacier and now covered with a multitude of small mobile dwellings and other buildings, almost in the style of a boom town, which would be swept away as the city was rebuilt.

She entered a saloon to which the compass led her, and went to a table in a quiet corner and seated herself, ordering a restorative drink from the waiter. No intoxicants were sold. Alcohol had been banned for some time, but some other drinks had arisen, scientifically formulated to simulate it without deleterious side effects.

The needle pointed directly to a man standing at the bar consuming a green liquid, and yet the man did not in the least resemble Sefner Quorne, except perhaps in height. He was bulky, massive-shouldered.

The Amazon lowered her gaze again and sat trying to puzzle the mystery out. After a moment or two, she became aware that a stranger had settled down at her table. He was a big, heavy-set fellow.

He spoke to her but she did not respond.

"I'm talking to yuh!" the man snapped. "Yuh don't have to sit there like a blasted dummy, do yuh?"

"Do you know that man at the bar with the green drink in his hand?" she asked.

The man glanced toward him. "Never seen him before. Why? What's the interest? In case you don't know it, I've claimed yuh for the moment."

The Amazon gazed at him, her lips setting. The contact lenses prevented him seeing the danger glint in her eyes. Suddenly his big hand reached out and tore the cap from her head, releasing the tumbling gold of her hair.

"What hair!" he said. "Yuh must be crazy ter hide it under a cap like that—"

"You infernal idiot!" the Amazon blazed at him, as she saw that the man with the green drink was gazing at her fixedly. "Keep your hands off me!"

"Lay off, Joe!" somebody shouted. "I'll stake all I've got that that's the Golden Amazon you're talkin' to—"

The man with the green drink gave a noticeable start, his puffy face turned toward the girl She stared at him fixedly, then Joe had suddenly seized her in his powerful arms.

"Golden Amazon nothing!" he cried. "Just because she's got hair like her? It just ain't possible—"

Flattening her hands against his chest, the Amazon forced herself out of his grip, took a step back, then swung up her right fist with blurring speed. Joe's doubts as to her identity vanished at that moment. The blow he absorbed lifted him from his feet and he sailed over the top of the nearest table. Half stunned he crashed on the floor as the table broke beneath him.

Angrily the Amazon looked about her, but the man with the green drink had gone. The girl looked at her compass and raced to the door; in the distance, at the farther end of the little street, she just caught a glimpse of the unknown as he hurried round a comer.

She followed him, streaking along at the speed of a track runner, ignoring the astonished looks of the men and women she passed on the way.

Presently she gained more deserted regions. Her quarry was out of sight, but the compass guided her. She moved with less urgency now, realizing she could trust the instrument. No matter where the unknown went she could follow him—right to the end of the universe if need be. Also realizing there was no point any more in concealing her identity, her hopes of secrecy having been blasted sky high by the odious attentions of Joe, she removed the contact lenses from her eyes, slipped them in her pocket, and doffed her overalls, revealing her Amazon costume beneath. If she were caught in a corner, she would need her full vision and not the limited scope of the imprisoning lenses.

CHAPTER TEN
NEEDLE OF DEATH

Steadily, untiringly, like a tigress stalking her prey, she wandered in and out of the twining wildernesses of buildings and at last, as darkness was settling and the temporary lights began to gleam in the streets around her, she found the needle had become motionless and was pointing leftward and upward. Immediately she followed its direction and it took her to a roughly constructed rooming house of five storeys. Outside it the Amazon stopped and consulted the needle. It was pointing to a window on the fifth floor—so she looked for her means of ascent up the edifice's gloomy façade—and found it in the main corner girder that jutted out from the roughly built frontage.

As stealthily as a cat she climbed it, and then edged her way along the parapet, entirely unconcerned by the fifty-foot drop to the ground if she missed her hold. She peered into the room beyond.

It was lighted with a low-powered bulb, and the heavily built man with the thick neck was sprawled on the bed, apparently exhausted after his long perambulation. The Amazon kicked her foot through the glass and leaped down into the room.

Before the man on the bed had time to grasp what had happened, she had reached him. She stopped at the bedside, her hands ready for instant action. He lay looking up at her dazedly from fat-rimmed eyes.

"I don't understand it!" he declared blankly. "I could have sworn I'd shaken you off."

"You didn't, and you never will."

The Amazon considered him fixedly and his eyes shifted under the malignancy of her stare. Then it dawned on her that his eyes were heliotrope in shade. Instantly her left hand shot out and gripped his throat with fiendish pressure.

"So you are from Atlantis!" she breathed, leaning over him. "I knew the compass couldn't be mistaken—"

He lashed at her with something shaped like a hypodermic syringe. Its needle struck her outthrust arm, into the flesh. She winced momentarily and felt a trickle of blood, then with her right hand she seized the syringe and flung it savagely on the floor, where it splintered.

Her briefly diverted attention was sufficient to allow the man to attempt to break free. He half got off the bed, then was slammed back on it again as the girl shifted her hand and brought it down in a fist into his face.

The outcome astounded her for a moment. The face collapsed like a smashed plaster cast and revealed another face beneath it—the face of Sefner Quorne. The iron grip on his throat pinned him, the remains of the other face crumbling about him. With it went black hair and a bull neck.

"Synthesis!" the Amazon said bitterly, holding him rigidly. "I was a fool not to think of it. Perhaps I would have only I understood from Abna that the Atlanteans do not understand synthesis."

"But they do," Quorne assured her "What they do not understand is how to breathe life into it, whereas you do." He shifted uncomfortably. "You are an intelligent woman, Miss Brant, and I have occupied a high position in the affairs of my race. Can we not talk a little more—comfortably?"

The Amazon reflected for a moment and then withdrew her grip, but she remained wary. Quorne made no further attempt to attack her. Raising himself, he pulled away the remains of his disguise.

"I really must congratulate you, Miss Brant. I don't know how you found me, unless it had something to do with the compass you just mentioned. I fully believed you had been flung into the sun along with Abna and the others in that space-globe. However, I must confess I was a trifle puzzled when I realized the beam was no longer operative. I could only assume you had been driven ahead of the beam, perhaps drawn by the solar gravity. Apparently not, since you are back on Earth."

"So is Abna. So are all of us. Never mind how we eluded you. What are you doing here? What is your aim? How did you arrive on Earth ahead of us?"

"A simple matter of instantaneous transportation. You have used the method yourself many a time to move quickly from place to place. So has Abna."

"I cannot think how you had the time to do it once we had penetrated the dome and allowed the ammoniated atmosphere to enter it."

"That too, Miss Brant, has a simple explanation," Quorne smiled coldly. "The moment I saw what had happened I sealed myself in my laboratory. There was time for that. The poison air took some little while to fill the great area under the dome. From my laboratory I deliberately smashed an area of the dome with a force beam when I saw that the rest of my race had perished. I planned to instantly transport myself to Atlantis—or what remained of it, according to Abna— and succeeded finally in working out the exact position, a complicated task over such a distance. The dome would have prevented my progress by blocking the necessary 'patterning' beam with my atoms in it, hence my destruction of part of it. I reintegrated in Atlantis, as I had calculated, and it was an easy task to resurrect some of the machines—one of them in particular which generated a force beam.

"All I had to do, through the telescope, was watch for your *Ultra* and fling it sunward as you approached Earth. Instead, you anchored it at the space-globe and I saw you all go within it. I then did my best to rid of you—without success, it would seem. Fully believing I had disposed of you, I disguised myself with synthetic tissue produced by the Atlantean machines, and became one of the workers of Earth here in this city."

"How did you get here?" The Amazon frowned.

"And why choose London?"

Quorne smiled faintly. "How? The same method I used to get to Atlantis from Jupiter—matter transmission. As I told you, I resurrected several of the most useful Atlantean machines. Monitoring of radio and television broadcasts soon told me that London was your capital city, and so I came here to pursue my plans. Shortly afterward, I learned of the descent of Atlantis into the sea once more. I could not quite understand it, and I had no facilities here for telescopic observation to see if the space-globe had, by some inexplicable process, returned. It was a blow to me, losing Atlantis. With it went the machines with which I had planned to conquer this planet."

"I do not understand," the Amazon said, "why you had to disguise yourself as a worker here in order to conquer the planet. You had the equipment in Atlantis to do it without moving from the spot."

"Not altogether. I found many of the most important machines had deteriorated with the tremendous lapse of time. To put them to rights I needed electrical equipment and other impedimenta, which I could only get in the outer world. So, I came here after disguising myself. I had hardly taken over the position of a worker before I realized Atlantis was lost. Not that it matters," Quorne finished, shrugging. "If I cannot rule this race, I can at least destroy it—and I have already started doing so."

"Which, if I read your deliberately blanked thoughts aright, has something to do with that needle you jammed into me," the Amazon snapped. "What was in it?"

Quorne only smiled; then his smile vanished at a stinging slap in the face.

"Answer the question! I'm not talking to myself."

"I'm not answering anything," he retorted.

"You'll discover what was in that syringe soon enough and by then it will be too late, I think—"

With one tremendous sweep of her arm the Amazon whirled the ex-adviser from the bed and flung him violently against the wall. Her hand at his throat was sufficient to hold him. In any case he was not a powerful man.

"I'm not going to argue with you, Quorne," the girl stated flatly. "I'm going to kill you, here and now, because 1 believe that is the safest thing for everybody. A man of your criminal tendencies and scientific skill is too dangerous to remain alive."

The girl's left hand joined her right and with relentless pressure she squeezed her fingers into the adviser's throat. He gasped and choked hopelessly, struggling to break loose, but could not dislodge the steel grip of the superwoman.

At last he was forced to the floor, his cadaverous face purple. Only when he relaxed did the Amazon release her hold. She looked down at him contemptuously and stooped to examine him; then she paused at a sudden knocking at the door.

"Mr. Baylis!" a woman's voice called out. "I've brought your supper, Mr. Baylis—!"

The Amazon swung and darted for the window, vanishing in the same silence with which she had arrived.

* * * * * * *

She returned to her headquarters in the administrative building to find Abna in consultation with Chris Wilson. They both looked up in the brilliance of the cold-light globes as she came in.

"After a great deal of trouble I managed to locate our friend Sefner Quorne," she explained, coming to the desk and sitting down.

"Then it *was* he!" Abna exclaimed.

"It was—very nicely disguised with synthetic tissue—" and the girl added the details of her adventure.

"Which takes care of him," Chris observed in satisfaction. "Altogether it seems we've removed all opposition from our midst, Vi, and can go straight ahead with this rebuilding job. I've arranged matters with Abna here, and he's taking charge of several scientific issues that are outside your scope. I've also assigned a suite to him in this administrative building."

"Good," the Amazon said absently; then she frowned. "I wish I knew what Quorne used when he stabbed me with that needle. I think I'd better make an examination of myself. I'll see you later."

"Come over to my home, Vi," Chris called after her, as she rose and headed for the office door. "I think it's time we had a reunion dinner, Abna included. We've quite a few things to celebrate."

"Very well," the girl nodded, and glanced at the clock. "I'll be at your home at eight."

She went on her way and to her own quarters. She spent half an hour changing and removing the grey composition from her skin, then exquisitely dressed in preparation for her dinner engagement, she departed once more, detouring on her way to her laboratory.

Locking herself in she went to a clinical cabinet and removed a testing needle. With it she extracted a drop of blood from the inside of her forearm and captured it on a microscopic slide; then she set to work examining it through high-powered lenses.

Despite every known test she could give it with reagents, there was apparently nothing wrong. Puzzled, she studied the tiny puncture where Quorne had jabbed the needle.

There did not appear to be any signs of inflammation. As a final test she X-rayed herself and measured heartbeats, blood pressure, and temperature. All recorded normally.

"Maybe water," she decided, with a grim smite, wiping the traces of the puncture from her arms. "Be just like Quorne to use water and leave the rest to imagination."

She drove her car to Chris Wilson's outer London home to find that he, Abna, Ethel, and Barry Schofield were already present, together with the two men and two women who had been through the Jovian adventure.

"I don't quite know what suits you best Vi," Abna commented as he surveyed her and smiled. "That superb gown you are wearing, or the robes of a queen."

She returned his survey. He was attired in immaculate evening dress, which made his big figure seem even larger.

"Let's just call ourselves civilians, Abna, shall we, and forget the rest? Oh, hello, Bee," the Amazon broke off, as her foster sister—Chris' wife—came into the room. "Some time since we were together."

"Far too long," Beatrice responded. "You never stay put for long, Vi."

The Amazon smiled and passed no comment. The conversation drifted into generalities in which she took no part. Then she found Abna beside her as she settled in a deep armchair.

"From what I hear," he said, "Ethel and Barry intend to be married next week."

"I'm sure they're admirably suited to each other," the Amazon responded. "Being married will perhaps cure Ethel of her tendency to constantly risk her neck in some mad exploit or other."

"You should talk!" Abna commented drily.

"It's different for me, Abna, and you know it: Ethel's a normal, happy girl with no particular talent for getting out of a corner, and certainly not the strength. I'm no ordinary woman."

"Which is a sore point with you?"

"Sometimes."

"It makes no difference to me, you know," he said.

"If it comes to that, I'm hardly a lounge-lizard myself. In all honesty, I can't see that I can do any more to conform to that you require of me. I am in your government; I've renounced all Atlantean rights. For every practical purpose I'm a young man asking you to marry me. Why not make the party really happy by accepting me?"

"We've been through all this before, Abna, and I'm not altering my decision. I'm too individual to marry. I want you as a friend, and there I prefer to stop."

"I can read thoughts as easily as you can when I want, you know," he reminded her. "I've been aware for some time that scientist in you is fighting with the woman. You'd be a fool to let cold-blooded science get the better of your natural instincts."

The Amazon hesitated, seemed on the verge of saying something, and then turned as the butler appeared in the doorway.

"Dinner is served...."

* * * * * * *

Apparently Abna had said all he intended in regard to himself and the Amazon, for in the week that followed he made no further reference to the subject. In any case he was kept busy devising new scientific plans to help in the rebuilding of London and the world in general—and the girl for her part was working tirelessly in the laboratory to devise plans for both colonizing the larger moons of Jupiter—giving them a breathable atmosphere—and using the space-globe as a halfway refueling and rest centre on the Earth-Mars run.

At the end of the week Ethel and Barry Schofield were married and went to tropical climes for their honeymoon.

Then, first in isolated instances and presently assuming the form of an epidemic, came disturbing news concerning the women workers engaged in countless occupations in rebuilding London.

One morning Chris Wilson said to the Amazon in his office: "Something's radically wrong. Last Monday I received a report that some twenty women had gone off on sick leave. This morning I hear that every one of them has died! On top of that another 120 women and girls are reported sick this morning."

Abna was present, and he said: "I think I should point out, Vi, that the women of the Atlantean race died in the same way! First in dozens, then hundreds, then thousands, until there was not a woman left."

"And you think it may be the same here?" the Amazon asked.

"It's a reasonable assumption, knowing that Quorne has been present. He knew where the bacillus was kept in the laboratories back home. He could easily have brought it with him when he came to Earth, and have turned it loose! He had only to introduce it into the bloodstream of one woman, and the damage would be done. It's exceptionally contagious, but only the female is attacked, human or animal."

The Amazon's eyes narrowed. "Now I know what

he meant when he said that if he couldn't rule the race he could at least destroy it. And he also said that he had already started doing so— That syringe!" she finished, snapping her fingers.

Chris Wilson gave her an anxious look. "What! You don't mean the one he stabbed into you? If that were true you'd be dead by now."

"That depends on my constitution," she answered. "I would not react as rapidly—if it all—as a normal woman. I've kept a check on myself and found nothing wrong—it's all clear now," she went on bitterly. "Quorne evidently brought that bacillus with him and only used it when he found he could no longer have Atlantis by which to gain control. When he lost everything, he decided to take revenge by destroying the race—which he will if women die." She got up quickly. "We'd better go and see these women who have been stricken and make sure it isn't something else."

Abna and Chris Wilson with her, she summoned an air taxi that took them to a hospital and they saw the stricken workers and heard the reports of the doctors. When they returned to the main office of the administrative building, they looked at each other grimly.

"It's it, right enough," Abna muttered. "And it will travel like wildfire now it has a hold. There are far too many people affected for me to cure them by mind force, otherwise I would."

"But there's an antidote!" the Amazon exclaimed. "Sefner Quorne himself said as much. You must know of it, Abna."

He became moodily silent. "Yes, there is one, which we found too late to save our women. But I don't know its composition. My father created it. Unless Quorne took it with him, it is in the surgical laboratory on Jupiter."

"Which means we had better try to find an antidote for ourselves if we are ever to do in time," the Amazon said. "In which you can't help me, Abna?"

"Unfortunately, no. I can only start from scratch the same as you. I think the better plan would be for me to return to Jupiter immediately, and try to find the antidote and bring it here."

"While you are doing that the disease will have made vast inroads," the Amazon reminded him.

"Not if I use instantaneous transportation, as I will in an emergency like this."

"There seems to be no other course," the girl admitted after reflection. "I'd go myself, only I wouldn't know where to look when I got there."

She led the way to the laboratory.

"Fortunately," she said, as she crossed to the complicated electronic equipment, which would make instantaneous transportation possible. "This apparatus of mine is already built. It is only a matter of calculating the path and the distance. The computers can do that."

She turned to the mathematical machines and then hesitated, a hand to her forehead. She felt a curious sensation of strain pass through her and die away almost immediately. It blurred her vision for a moment and she staggered giddily. Instantly Abna had an arm about her.

"What's wrong, Vi?" he asked in surprise. "Not feeling well?"

She laughed shortly. "I'm all right: just a little disorder for a second."

She turned to the computer and programmed it in action so that it would give the required information for the trip to Jupiter. Abna spent the interval getting into a heavy spacesuit, and fitting it with a variety of weapons and instruments on its belt. He left the helmet on its hinge, unscrewed, until the last moment.

"Here it is," the girl said at last, and took a printout from the machine, upon which was detailed the information she wanted. Working from its data, she set the equipment and then stood aside, motioning to the transmitting plate.

"Ready?" Abna asked, and as she nodded he stepped forward into the area of the machine's huge transmission magnets.

"I'm not an appreciative person as a rule, I suppose," the Amazon commented, "but I realize what you are doing for us in making this trip, Abna. You're risking your life so that the women of this race can be saved. I'm grateful for it."

"Later, perhaps, you will show your gratitude in a more practical way," he commented; then, before she could speak again he dropped his helmet in position and raised a gloved hand to indicate that he was ready.

The girl closed the switch and stood watching the uncanny effect of him slowly dissolving into nothing as his whole body and attire was changed into an atomic pattern. Then he was gone, the instruments showing that the pattern was being hurled at the speed of light along its appointed course.

The girl sat down to watch the controls. The instant the master-gauge touched zero it meant that Abna had reached Jupiter. There he would rematerialize and be allowed three hours in which to find the antidote. At the end of that period the apparatus, magnetically following him with its governor beams, would dematerialize him once more and return him to his starting point—with whatever he happened to have with him at the time. Recalling her own sensations upon occasions when she had performed a similar feat, the Amazon did not envy him.

Though it was not necessary for her to control the apparatus in any way, she could not help but watch it intently. It showed her exactly where the pattern of Abna was, and how he was faring. She was extremely anxious for his safety, far more so than she had admitted to him.

She stirred uncomfortably in her chair as a throbbing pain in her head made itself evident. Physical disorders were so utterly unknown to her that she had no tolerance for anything that caused her a moment's discomfort. Rising, she started to go to the clinical instrument case, but she did not reach it. Abruptly she felt herself sliding incredibly, and a cloud of varicoloured stars seemed to burst before her eyes. She found she was lying on her face, hardly able to move hand or foot.

"Chris!" she called weakly. "Chris—!"

From the office he heard her and came hurrying in, plainly amazed at the sight of her lying helpless on the floor.

"Chris," she whispered. "I seem to be getting the same way as other women. Get me some of that X-42 essence. In the cupboard there."

Chris obeyed with nervous speed, and the drink appeared to have an effect, for after a moment or two she straightened up.

"That's better," she said in relief, and raised her eyes to look at him as he stood beside her. "No use blinking the fact, Chris. I've got the same trouble as the rest of the dying women on this planet. I've no doubts now but what Quorne dosed me pretty thoroughly when he jammed that needle into me. I can perhaps ward it off until Abna gets back with the antidote. It'll mean constant dosing with this superessence. I've got to keep on living!"

"You're sure a doctor couldn't help?"

The girl smiled cynically. "Hardly! I know more than all the doctors put together. I have one advantage—an extremely strong constitution with which I may be able to hold out. Otherwise I expect I'd have gone under long before this."

Chris went, making no effort to disguise his anxiety. The Amazon walked slowly back to the clinical cabinet and spent some time conducting an analysis of herself. This time, instead of everything being normal, she found everything the opposite. Too weary to bother analyzing the details, she went back to the transmission equipment and sat down before it. The needle on the master gauge had touched zero, satisfying her that Abna had reached the end of his long journey.

Indeed, at that moment he was materializing inside his spacesuit under the swirling clouds of the giant planet. As he looked about him and recovered from the intense physical anguish of reintegration he realized that timing had been amazingly accurate. He was no more than a quarter of a mile from the giant dome, a gaping fissure dimly visible in it at ground level where, presumably, Sefner Quorne had blasted a way through for himself. The hole in the summit, which the *Ultra* had used to make its departure to Earth, was still there.

Moving with stupendous effort in the vast gravitation, Abna began to advance, dragging his feet as he went. It took him all of an hour to reach the crack in the dome. He eased himself through it, taking infinite care that the jagged edges did not rip his spacesuit.

Here, within the dome, the gravity was back to normal, for the machines were still running under their own power and counteracting the terrific pull. The lights had failed, however, so with only his powerful flashlight to guide him, he made his way through the silent upper reaches and so gradually reached the city. Here, a lone figure, he walked along the main street, considering the dead bodies of the Atlanteans sprawled in all manner of postures, stricken by the deadly poison of the atmosphere.

He reached the laboratories to find them intact.

Quickly he hurried to the department where various chemicals were stored. He instantly detected two gaps in the orderly rows of vials upon the shelves. He frowned as he examined them at close quarters. The gap, he knew, had contained the sealed bacillus, which had been isolated as the cause of killing all the women in the race; the other had contained the antidote, its exact formula unknown to him, except that he knew it was steeped in ammoniated salts to preserve its potency.

The mental shock of finding the stuff gone after his 400-million mile leap across space was stupendous. Frantically he searched the shelves, flinging aside the useless chemicals in his anxiety. All the time he kept thinking of Sefner Quorne. Evidently as well as taking the bacillus, the sinister adviser had also taken the antidote. Yet this hardly seemed logical. Why should he need to take something to stop the disease when his only aim, apparently, had been to start it when all else failed?

"Hello there!"

Abna distinctly heard somebody call to him cheerfully. Realizing how impossible this was through his helmet, he suddenly remembered the Jovian gift of telepathy. Swinging around, he flashed his torch beam until it settled on a squat, broad-as-long figure with a grey-scaled body sitting indolently against the wall and grinning. The bright yellow eyes reflected the torchlight.

"You!" Abna exclaimed, starting, and his thoughts

reached the squat Jovian for he nodded.

"That's right. Same fellow you met before when you couldn't get inside the dome. I supposed you managed it all right? But I see from your thoughts that you did."

Abna did not speak or concentrate on anything at that moment. He was fascinated by the fact that the Jovian had a vial in his scaly hand and was drinking from it in profound satisfaction, munching contentedly as crystals cracked between his pointed teeth.

"Hey!" Abna yelled in horror, and his thoughts must have been violent, for the Jovian started under the impact of it. He lowered the bottle and stared. Abna dived for it, but he was not quick enough to yank it from the Jovian's hand. He put it behind his back.

"What's wrong, Earthman?" he asked curiously. "Why do you want to take a good meal away from me? I haven't had such lovely stuff since the day I was born. Really refined crystals and a fluid like the rarest wine. It's a pity you can't appreciate it—"

"That's an antidote!" Abna yelled inside his helmet. "It's the cure for a blight which destroyed all the females in my race."

"Is it?" the Jovian grinned. "It's good stuff, anyway. If it comes to that, there's a lot of good stuff in this place. I have been looking around since I found the dome had been smashed open. Quite a treasure trove— so much so I don't want my wife or any of my friends to know about it. They'd eat the place up."

He brought the vial into view again and before Abna could stop him, tipped the remaining contents into his wide mouth and chewed happily. Dazed, Abna stared at him through his helmet vizor, and was rewarded by a mischievous wink from one heavily lidded eye.

CHAPTER ELEVEN
ABNA RETURNS

For three hours, drinking essence at intervals to maintain her strength, the Amazon remained beside the transmission machine, waiting until it should start up again automatically and bring Abna back to Earth. It was mid-afternoon when the time was up and with a sudden click a soft whirring of power announced that the machine was in operation again. Heavy-eyed, the Amazon studied the readings and found everything satisfactory.

Then she glanced up as Chris Wilson came in, his face betraying his deep anxiety.

"How much longer is Abna likely to be?" he asked.

"Not long now. He's on his way back—or should be unless something has gone radically wrong. Why?"

"It's Ethel." Chris moved restlessly. "Barry just phoned me that the disease is as rife in the tropics as it is here— presumably carried by airliner passengers from here. Ethel's ill—desperately so."

The Amazon got to her feet, steadying herself against the bench.

She said, frowning: "All she can do for the moment

is take X-42 essence. It should keep her going until Abna returns. He can't be very long now. Phone Barry right away and tell him what to do."

At last the time was up and Abna was due to reappear on the transmission plate.

Nothing happened. The Amazon stared fixedly as the power began to decline, its term of life brought automatically to a close. Slowly a dead silence fell on the laboratory.

"It can't be!" she whispered, commencing a hasty check over the instruments. "He must come back! He's got to!"

The instruments were correct: no doubt of that. There seemed little doubt but what Abna had reached Jupiter safely and rematerialized, but what had happened after that the girl had no idea. He should have been brought back, even if dead. Only a flaw in mathematics that might have disintegrated him in space, or some kind of barrier which would prevent the return beam functioning properly, could explain the mystery.

All she could do was send forth a second return beam in the hope that it might function where its predecessor presumably had not. The equipment she set to operate at two-hour intervals. Somehow it might yet recall Abna and, apart from actually travelling to Jupiter to check up on things for herself, this was all she could do.

Bemused, she left the laboratory and went into the main office. Chris looked at her intently.

"Well?" he asked. "Where is he?"

"Lost," she answered dully. "I don't understand it. If he can come back, he will. I've left a return beam in permanent focus that will dissemble and return him."

"But what happens now?" Chris demanded, getting up and coming over to her. "Vi, for heavens' sake try and understand this situation! Look at my desk there! Reports of women dying the world over—in thousands. Dropping at their work, in the streets, in their homes— In a few more hours there'll be a staggering death roll. They're calling out to you for help. Something's got to be done!"

"How's Ethel?" the girl asked moodily.

"She's taken some X-42 and it's revived her for the time being. Obviously, though, she can't keep on doing that. I'd fly over and see her but I couldn't do her any good. Barry's doing what he can."

The Amazon said: "I can't deal with something I don't understand. I'm half dead myself, in case you don't realize it. Certainly I can't think or work out plans. Unless Abna comes back, this thing will have to run its course."

Chris stared at her. "What? And allow every woman on the planet to die?"

"The Atlanteans had that frightful fact to accept when their science was powerless: so must we, for my science is far behind theirs.... But the race won't be destroyed, Chris. I have one secret which the Atlanteans had not got—living synthesis."

Chris still gazed numbly, brought face to face with the stunning comprehension that the all-powerful

Golden Amazon had not the energy or even the ability to defeat the doom that was striking down her and the entire female race.

"Even if I die," she continued listlessly, "as I shall; even if every woman vanishes from the scheme of things, synthesis can master the problem. Beings who will obey the orders of the men who are left. Possibly synthetic women will be immune to this disease. If so, there is the basis of a new race."

"It's horrible," Chris muttered. "Even more horrible that you of all people should contemplate it. I always thought you could master any problem if you worked at it long enough."

The girl sat down heavily.

"Normally, perhaps I could—but the urge has gone, Chris." She gave him a hunted look. "I'm dying, I know I am. And though I hate to admit it, there's only one person can save me and the rest of the women—and that's Abna. What a glorious chance for him to lord it over me!"

"He wouldn't do that," Chris told her. "He's not that kind of man."

* * * * * * *

For several seconds after the grinning Jovian had swallowed the last of the contents of the antidote bottle, Abna stood staring at him. Then he strode forward angrily.

"Why the excitement?" the Jovian asked.

"Why?" Abna yelled inside his helmet, and his

thoughts battered so that the creature winced. "I've travelled all this distance from Earth to get that antidote and you consume it! Isn't that enough to send anybody crazy?"

"What makes you think there's only one antidote?" the Jovian inquired, getting to his feet. "There's tons of it all around us."

Abna looked about him in the torchlight and shook his head. "You're wrong!" he snapped. "There was only one antidote, and that was it."

"I can tell you exactly what it was made of," the Jovian explained, quite unconcerned. "My palate is capable of analyzing whatever touches it, and the percentages thereof. We have a higher sense of taste than you. The antidote was made up of various ingredients, comprising—" He hesitated and then gave them, each one a chemical vaguely familiar to Abna but unknown in Earth chemistry. "And the whole substance was preserved in chloride of ammonium and other ammoniacal salts. Anyway," the Jovian grinned, "it's a simple matter to make some more. Come over here."

Infinitely relieved, Abna followed the squat, powerful creature to the bench, and then stood watching in wonder as with superlative skill he measured out various quantities of chemicals from the bottles on the shelves. Apparently laboratory work came naturally to him. It seemed even queerer to Abna that a creature with such outstanding gifts could have no ambition to develop them and master his planet—yet there it was.

The Jovians had no spark of enterprise whatever.

An hour drifted into two—then three. Abna still remained holding his torch and looking on. By this time the Jovian had filled three large vials with the antidote, complete with their protective ammonium crystals.

"It's a real sacrifice for me to hand these over and not eat them," he confessed. "Still, I suppose it must be so. There is enough stuff in this laboratory to satisfy me for a long time to come. Do you think you'll have enough of the stuff here?"

"More than enough," Abna assured him. "It only takes a 100th of a drop to each woman who is dying. There's enough here to deal with all of them. If there isn't, I can always come back—"

"But you can't be sure of finding me," the Jovian reminded him. "I might be anywhere. I do think you'll have enough—" His thoughts ceased for a moment as he noticed Abna glancing about him worriedly. "Something troubling you, Earthman?"

"Yes. I just remembered how much time has gone past. A beam should have dematerialized me and returned me to Earth long before this. I can't imagine why it hasn't."

"I can," the Jovian said pleasantly, and Abna swung on him.

"Why? For heavens' sake tell me! If that beam doesn't function, I'm stranded here, unless I can get the transportation apparatus going in this laboratory."

"You won't. The poison in the atmosphere has

corroded most of the wirings: I've already checked it. However, the reason no beam has reacted on you is because you're inside this dome. Nothing, not even radiation, will penetrate it from outside—or had you forgotten that?"

"Yes, I had," Abna admitted, startled. "Of course! The beam will only react on me without any negative field intervening. I'd better get out quickly and see if by any chance the beam is still there." He swept up the three vials and hurried away.

* * * * * * *

In her laboratory, the Amazon sat, considering a synthetic woman as she walked slowly up and down the centre aisle between the instrument benches. She was attired in overalls and had face and figure scale-made, though not resembling any particular person. In general, the Amazon had created her from a composite of the best features of most women, avoiding all resemblance to herself. The 'patterner', which contained her own image, was locked away and only used when vitally necessary. Power given to a superior Golden Amazon was, as she knew, far too dangerous.

"She'll do," Chris Wilson said, as the woman, obeying the mental orders he himself was giving her, sat down mechanically. "You've done a nice job, Vi. If necessary, then all we have to do is create thousands of them in the image of this woman?"

"That's it," the girl agreed wearily. "Over there, in that machine, is everything you need. Now I'd better tell the people what is intended."

She switched on the radio apparatus and began speaking. She spoke in a voice quite unlike her own. It lacked force and vitality and was pitched in a dreary monotone. She outlined the facts concerning the growing deaths of women the world over, explained how the hope of an antidote had not materialized, and concluded with a statement of her decision to create synthetic women to take the place of the dying natural ones.

"An antidote may yet arrive," she said finally. "If it does, well and good. If it does not, the race will at least go on living. That is my hope. If it so happens that I die, too, at least have the satisfaction of knowing that I have done everything possible to keep our race alive."

With that she switched off and turned her burning eyes to look at Chris. His face was solemn.

"I just heard about Ethel," he said quietly. "Before I came here to see the synthetic woman. I didn't want to disturb you then—Ethel's going fast, Vi. She's taken all the restorative she can, and I'm afraid it's the finish."

"For all of us women, I'm afraid," the Amazon answered; then she forced herself from her chair and looked at the synthetic being. "She'll obey anybody's mental order and spoken words," she explained. "I've made her that way— Rise!" she commanded. "Leave here and mingle with the people. Go to the labour centre and report yourself as Synthetic Number One. Take your instructions from there and follow them out."

The woman remained motionless. The Amazon frowned and repeated the order. Then she went forward and examined the creature carefully. At last she stood back, quivering with ironic laughter.

"What is it?" Chris asked sharply.

"She's dead!" the Amazon cried hoarsely. "Dead! I brought her to life with cosmic radiation and the disease has struck her down before she can even start. Probably she contracted it from me as I made her. She's as vulnerable as a natural woman. We're beaten, Chris! We're beaten—"

With that her vast reserves gave way at last and she sagged helplessly in Chris' grip, yet as she did so she could have sworn she had seen Abna for a moment, materializing out of the air near the still-humming transmission machine. Unconsciousness swamped her before she could be sure.

* * * * * *

Her next realization was of looking at a high corner of the ceiling of her bedroom. By degrees she appreciated the fact that it was evening and a mellow breeze was stirring the curtains at the open window. She felt neither ill nor well: just in a suspended in-between state. She moved her gaze to look through the window toward the stars just commencing to gleam.

"If I am to die," she whispered, "I could wish nothing better than to be allowed to roam out there forever, once I have cast this fleshy form—" Tears misted her eyes for a moment. "But I do not want to die so soon, with so little done—"

"You're not going to die, Vi."

The girl was too weak to move anything but her head. Her eyes settled on the figure of Abna standing at the bedside. He looked tired, for him, and the suit he was wearing was travel-stained.

"Abna!" the Amazon breathed. "Oh—thank God! You came back after all. I thought I'd lost you! What happened?"

"It was my own fault. I was inside the force dome on Jupiter and it blocked the return beams."

"I shall never cease to be grateful for leaving the beam on just in case—the antidote! Did you get it?"

"I got it," he assented, then before he could speak further, the girl broke in on him again.

"Cure Ethel, Abna! Cure her before anybody else. If only you will, I'll marry you. I promise I will."

Abna looked down at her curiously. "With no race to perpetuate, Vi, where's the point in it?"

"It's what you want, isn't it?"

"It always has been. But is it what you want?"

The girl was silent. With a smile, Abna stooped and kissed her.

"It's taken a long time for the woman to beat the scientist," he said gravely. "But you'll never regret it, Vi. Never. Now, give me your arm."

He took it in his powerful hand as it lay relaxed on the coverlet. The Amazon winced momentarily as a needle stabbed, and for a moment or two she felt no change; then very gradually she realized that the deadness was leaving her limbs, that her heart was beating more rapidly, that the clouds were clearing from her brain. The hollowness of her features began to fill out and brighter lights came into her fine eyes.

"That's better," Abna nodded, and sitting on the bed edge, he put an arm about her shoulder and raised her. For a moment or two she remained motionless, her tumbled golden hair about his arm. Then suddenly she flung back her head, her eyes challenging his. He saw in them the old Amazonian gleam, the determination in her set mouth.

"Why are you stopping here?" she demanded, pushing herself away from him. "I've said I'll marry you, and I will. But cure Ethel and then help the other women who—"

She broke off, staring in amazement as Abna chuckled. She was on the point of demanding an explanation when the bedroom door suddenly opened and, dumbfounded, the Amazon gazed at Ethel and Barry Schofield, both of them looking the picture of health. Only a pace or two behind them came Chris Wilson and his wife.

Feeling completely revitalized, the Amazon sat up.

"I thought—" she began to say blankly; then Abna cut her short.

"I landed back on Earth, Vi, just as you became unconscious. Chris told me of Ethel's condition, so I went to her first and revived her, bringing her back here. I was satisfied that your great strength would give you at least a week's more life. Then I distributed the antidote with full instructions, and finally came here. I revived you last of all. Your promising to marry me if I cured Ethel was your own idea, remember. I accepted for one reason—to show that I really do love you. Having no race to think about any more, what other reason could I have for wanting to make you my wife...? I think I can safely say that in a week womanhood will be back to normal and the bacillus which caused the trouble will have been isolated and destroyed."

The Amazon said nothing. She had rarely looked so completely astonished.

"This means," she said at last, "that you've beaten me!"

"You beat yourself, Vi. I didn't have anything to do with it."

For just a moment longer the hardness remained about her mouth, then it relaxed into a rueful smile.

"I spoke out of turn," she admitted. "But I don't regret it, Abna. Nothing else would ever have made me break down and say what I really wanted to say—"

She turned as a maid came in and handed the Amazon a letter.

"A special messenger just brought this, Miss Brant," she explained and went out.

The Amazon read the letter in gathering amazement, then aloud:

"It's dated today and simply says 'London'. Then it goes on":

"'Dear Miss Brant: I must congratulate you on having counteracted the bacillus with which

I felt sure I could exterminate this race, but I do not intend to be so easily defeated. I have little regard for you or his late highness Abna, and my ambition still remains to use my science to master this solar system if at all possible.

"'I have added a quota of energy to my body which destroys my former aura-radiation reading, so you will not be able to find me. This is an indication of the scientific power I possess. After you tried to strangle me, my landlady revived me, and I gave her an excuse for my earlier disguise—that I was hiding from an assailant who had finally caught up with me! You will remember you did not have the time to properly examine me, otherwise you would found my heart still beating. I look forward to renewing our acquaintance on terms that must of necessity be advantageous to me. Sincerely yours,

Sefner Quorne'.'"

The Amazon lowered the letter and met Abna's eyes. He reflected for a moment and then smiled.

"Just as well you did promise to marry me, Vi," he decided. "To beat Quorne we are going to need every wit and resource we both possess!"

ABOUT THE AUTHOR

British writer JOHN RUSSELL FEARN was born near Manchester, England, in 1908. As a child he devoured the science fiction of Wells and Verne, and was a voracious reader of the Boys' Story Papers. He was also fascinated by the cinema, and first broke into print in 1931 with a series of articles in *Film Weekly*.

He then quickly sold his first novel, *The Intelligence Gigantic*, to the American magazine, *Amazing Stories*. Over the next fifteen years, writing under several pseudonyms, Fearn became one of the most prolific contributors to all of the leading US science fiction pulps, including such legendary publications as *Astounding Stories*, *Startling Stories*, *Thrilling Wonder Stories*, and *Weird Tales*.

During the late 1940s he diversified into writing novels for the UK market, and also created his famous superwoman character, The Golden Amazon, for the prestigious Canadian magazine, the Toronto *Star Weekly*. In the early 1950s in the UK, his fifty-two novels as "Vargo Statten" were bestsellers, most notably his novelization of the film, *Creature from the Black Lagoon*.

Apart from science fiction, he had equal success with westerns, romances, and detective fiction, writing an amazing total of 180 novels—most of them in a period of just ten years—before his early death in 1960. His work has been translated into nine languages, and continues to be reprinted and read worldwide.

www.ingramcontent.com/pod-product-compliance
Lightning Source LLC
Chambersburg PA
CBHW050738250626
47155CB00005B/1831